A CHANGE OF HEARTS

When they entered the Church she saw the Marquis standing at the lectern turning over the pages of the large Bible.

Neisa felt a sudden and unusual excitement rising within her that she could not control.

The Marquis looked so handsome and she realised that reading the lesson was important to him – it was what few young gentlemen of such distinction would feel.

'He is a very remarkable man,' she told herself.

She and Lady Sarah entered the family pew.

As they knelt to pray, Neisa admitted to herself that she loved the Marquis.

She had given him both her heart and soul.

She had not intended to.

She had known only too well, as the Viscountess had told her, that it was just hopeless for her to fall in love with anyone from a different world to her own.

She could well understand that the Marquis would not want to be married until he was a great deal older.

He wanted to enjoy himself as most men would.

Beautiful ladies like the Viscountess all fawned on him and, Neisa pondered, were only too willing to fall into his arms.

She felt, as she ruminated about it, as if she had stabbed herself and the knife had made a hole in her heart.

THE BARBARA CARTLAND PINK COLLECTION

Titles in this series

A CHANGE OF HEARTS

BARBARA CARTLAND

Barbaracartland.com Ltd

ISBN 978-1-906950-09-5

Printed and bound in Great Britain by Cle-Print Ltd.
of St Ives, Cambridgeshire.

THE BARBARA CARTLAND PINK COLLECTION

Barbara Cartland was the most prolific bestselling author in the history of the world. She was frequently in the Guinness Book of Records for writing more books in a year than any other living author. In fact her most amazing literary feat was when her publishers asked for more Barbara Cartland romances, she doubled her output from 10 books a year to over 20 books a year, when she was 77.

She went on writing continuously at this rate for 20 years and wrote her last book at the age of 97, thus completing 400 books between the ages of 77 and 97.

Her publishers finally could not keep up with this phenomenal output, so at her death she left 160 unpublished manuscripts, something again that no other author has ever achieved.

Now the exciting news is that these 160 original unpublished Barbara Cartland books are already being published and by Barbaracartland.com exclusively on the internet, as the international web is the best possible way of reaching so many Barbara Cartland readers around the world.

The 160 books are published monthly and will be numbered in sequence.

The series is called the Pink Collection as a tribute to Barbara Cartland whose favourite colour was pink and it became very much her trademark over the years.

The Barbara Cartland Pink Collection is published only on the internet. Log on to www.barbaracartland.com to find out how you can purchase the books monthly as they are published, and take out a subscription that will ensure that all subsequent editions are delivered to you by mail order to your home.

NEW

Barbaracartland.com is proud to announce the publication of ten new Audio Books for the first time as CDs. They are favourite Barbara Cartland stories read by well-known actors and actresses and each story extends to 4 or 5 CDs. The Audio Books are as follows:

The Patient Bridegroom	The Passion and the Flower
A Challenge of Hearts	Little White Doves of Love
A Train to Love	The Prince and the Pekinese
The Unbroken Dream	A King in Love
The Cruel Count	A Sign of Love

More Audio Books will be published in the future and the above titles can be purchased by logging on to the website www.barbaracartland.com or please write to the address below.

If you do not have access to a computer, you can write for information about the Barbara Cartland Pink Collection and the Barbara Cartland Audio Books to the following address:

Barbara Cartland.com Ltd., Camfield Place,
Hatfield, Hertfordshire AL9 6JE, United Kingdom.

Telephone: +44 (0)1707 642629
Fax: +44 (0)1707 663041

THE LATE DAME BARBARA CARTLAND

Barbara Cartland who sadly died in May 2000 at the age of nearly 99 was the world's most famous romantic novelist who wrote 723 books in her lifetime with worldwide sales of over 1 billion copies and her books were translated into 36 different languages.

As well as romantic novels, she wrote historical biographies, 6 autobiographies, theatrical plays, books of advice on life, love, vitamins and cookery. She also found time to be a political speaker and television and radio personality.

She wrote her first book at the age of 21 and this was called *Jigsaw*. It became an immediate bestseller and sold 100,000 copies in hardback and was translated into 6 different languages. She wrote continuously throughout her life, writing bestsellers for an astonishing 76 years. Her books have always been immensely popular in the United States, where in 1976 her current books were at numbers 1 & 2 in the B. Dalton bestsellers list, a feat never achieved before or since by any author.

Barbara Cartland became a legend in her own lifetime and will be best remembered for her wonderful romantic novels, so loved by her millions of readers throughout the world.

Her books will always be treasured for their moral message, her pure and innocent heroines, her good looking and dashing heroes and above all her belief that the power of love is more important than anything else in everyone's life.

"I have always said that you may change whatever you wish in life, but true love remains the same – pure, innocent and incredibly beautiful."

Barbara Cartland

CHAPTER ONE
1891

Neisa rang the bell of the impressive door of the house in Park Lane.

While she was waiting patiently, she looked down at the plant she held in her hand – it was just coming into bloom and was of a particularly rare species.

As it was a gift, she had put some coloured paper round it and tied it with a pink ribbon.

The door was opened by a footman and there was a butler standing just behind him.

"Is Miss Waverton at home?" enquired Neisa.

"She is, madam," the butler replied. "May I have your name?"

"I am Miss Neisa Moore."

The butler ushered her, with some pomposity, into an imposing sitting room near the front door.

It seemed to be filled with everything that money could buy and Neisa looked around with interest.

She wondered what it would feel like to be so rich that one could buy everything one wanted – not as she and her father had to do at present which was to count every penny.

Her father, the Reverend Patrick Moore had always lived in a state of penury and yet surprisingly he invariably got what he wanted in life.

He had fallen head over heals in love with a very ravishing girl when he had only just left Oxford.

Lady Elizabeth Stoner was the only daughter of a distinguished Earl who was finding it difficult to keep his ancestral home in existence.

He was therefore relying on his daughter Elizabeth, since she was so beautiful, to bring him a rich son-in-law.

Elizabeth was quite agreeable to do what her father wanted as being of a sweet and gentle nature, she preferred to do what she was told rather than think for herself.

Yet when she saw Patrick Moore she lost her head as well as her heart.

He was undoubtedly not only the most handsome young man she had ever met, but quite the most amusing and interesting.

Patrick had travelled South to London because his father wanted him to meet people who could be useful to him in the future.

He was always exceedingly busy and had no time to read newspapers, especially the Social columns in which he was not interested.

It was only when he returned North to stay with a friend that he met Elizabeth and they spent two evenings together in the company of their friends.

Then Patrick learned that she was being married the following day to an immensely rich German Baron, who, although getting on in life, had fallen for her beauty just as Patrick had.

As soon as he realised what was about to happen, Patrick went into immediate action.

All through his life he had been impulsive without thinking of the consequences, so he borrowed his friend's horses and carriage.

He then drove at a tremendous speed to where he was told the wedding was taking place.

The wedding had been arranged in a hurry as the German Baron wished to return to his own country.

When Patrick walked in through the West door, the Parson was already intoning,

"If any man can show any just cause why they may not lawfully be joined together in holy matrimony, let him now speak or hereafter forever hold his peace – "

"I forbid this marriage!" Patrick shouted.

Everyone in the Church turned round and there was a hushed silence as he walked up the aisle.

"I forbid this marriage," he boomed again, "because the bride is not in love with the man she is marrying, but with *me*."

Thinking he was some kind of lunatic, the Parson suggested calmly,

"I think we had now better retire to the vestry and discuss this matter quietly."

"There is nothing to discuss," cried Patrick, as he put out his right hand and took hold of Elizabeth's.

"I love you, Elizabeth, and I know you love me!"

She looked at him adoringly, knowing what he said was true.

She had wept every night since her father had told her that she was to marry the Baron.

One look into her eyes was enough for Patrick.

He did not wait, but holding onto Elizabeth's hand tightly, he ran down the aisle pulling her after him.

She did not resist.

Before anyone in the Church could do anything to stop them, Patrick had lifted the bride into his carriage and driven off at great speed.

The Earl was furious and attempted to follow the runaways.

They slipped over the Scottish border quietly and were married at once 'by consent' in the age-old method that is still legal in Scotland.

They then registered their marriage with the Sheriff and there was nothing the Earl could do about it.

He cut his daughter out of his life, refused to speak to her ever again and stopped the small allowance she had received from him in the past.

Patrick, although wildly happy, was faced with the problem of what he should do next.

Just how could he earn enough to keep his wife and perhaps later a family?

He had, when he was at Oxford University, vaguely thought of becoming a doctor.

He had learned first aid and a smattering of what he would require later for examinations. However, his most valuable asset was his boundless charm and good looks.

Because both he and Elizabeth wanted to get away from England, Patrick became what was called a 'Medical Missionary'.

The Mission he joined was prepared to send him to many parts of the world to expound the Gospel.

At the same time, the Mission had found from long experience that a missionary who could heal the sick was far more likely to win converts than one who could merely offer the natives words and prayers.

Patrick, accompanied by his beautiful wife, was an outstanding success.

They travelled to many strange countries in the East and spent some time in Africa with tribes who had not been known to the civilised world or even written about.

Patrick was able to convert a great many natives or so he believed.

Elizabeth wrote several reports and sent them back to England and they were so interesting and in some parts amusing that the Missionary Society had them printed.

When their little daughter was born they decided to call her Neisa, which means 'purity' in ancient Greek.

Her parents thought she was as beautiful as the love they had for each other.

The fact that Neisa was now an essential part of the Moore family made no difference to their life at all – they merely took her along with them wherever they went.

She learned to sleep comfortably in a cave, on the deck of a ship or in a tiny tent to protect all three of them from insects and unpleasant creatures of the night.

It was only when Elizabeth died of a virulent fever for which even Patrick could find no cure that he decided his wandering days were over and he must settle down.

He recognised that the story of his many adventures abroad would make an excellent series of books, not only because the Missionary Society had told him so, but so had Elizabeth.

He was going to have to write everything without any help and yet he knew that was what she would want him to do.

In the meantime Patrick's father had managed to procure for him the position of Vicar of the parish where the family house was situated.

The Old Manor had been in the possession of the Moores for over two hundred years and they were proud of it simply because it was theirs.

The family estate owned very little land and was in an isolated part of the country, but the villagers welcomed Patrick because they had known him since he was a boy.

As there were very few parishioners, he had plenty of time to write as he wished and he began by writing for the Missionary Society.

In fact, his only real problem was that he was short of money.

Then he was fortunate in having a book on travel accepted by a well-known publisher, but it did not make him a fortune.

However, it made enough to provide Neisa with a better education than he had been able to give her himself.

She had tutors in languages and was proficient in many subjects that girls of her age would not be taught.

It meant that, as her father was short of money, she was short of clothes.

But they were so happy in their small Vicarage that she did not complain.

Her aunt had meanwhile compensated for what her grandfather had considered a disgraceful and outrageous marriage.

She had married a man who was not titled, but well on the way to becoming very rich – he had many business contacts in America and had met the Earl quite by chance at a dinner party.

When he had been invited to stay at the attractive ancestral home of the Earl of Stoner, he then met the Earl's elder daughter Alice.

Just as Patrick had done with Elizabeth, he fell head over heels in love with her.

This time the Earl made certain that no one should interfere at the wedding and spirit the bride away.

He need not have worried as Alice was as much in love with Clive Waverton as he was with her.

They travelled to America after they were married,

and it was then many years later when they had returned to England for a long visit that Alice finally got in touch with Patrick Moore.

She wanted to hear about her sister's death and also attempt to heal the breach in the family.

What she discovered was that Patrick's daughter, Neisa, was almost the same age as her daughter Carol – in fact there were only a few months between them.

The two girls met and formed an immediate liking for each other.

However, Clive Waverton had too much at stake in America to stay for too long in England.

He also found that his wife's family and his father-in-law, who had grown old and rather grumpy, a bore.

So he returned to America.

And it was two years later before Patrick and his daughter Neisa learned that Alice had died in Colorado.

There was no question for the moment that Clive Waverton and Carol might return to England.

Then unexpectedly a month ago, Neisa received a letter from Carol saying that they were coming to London for the Season.

Carol wrote,

"*I am now eighteen, as you are, and Papa wishes me to meet with all the smart people in Society. So he has bought a large house in London where he will give a ball for me.*

Of course, I am expecting you to come to it, dearest Neisa, and it will be so lovely to see you again.

I have already received two proposals of marriage, and I wonder how many you have had!

I will tell you all about it when we meet, so please come to see me as soon as you can.

Affectionately,

Your cousin, Carol."

Neisa showed the letter to her father who remarked,

"Well, I expect Waverton will do things in style for his daughter, which is more, my dearest, than I can do for you."

"I know that Papa, but I am very happy, so do not worry, please."

She did not want to admit it, but she thought that it would be impossible for her to attend Carol's ball.

She did not own a smart evening gown and it would be unthinkable at present for her father to find the money for one.

They managed in the Vicarage with just the help of a woman who came in daily to clean the floors and do the washing.

Neisa did all the cooking and she knew better than anyone how difficult it was to make ends meet.

There was, however, always a scintilla of hope that her father's next book would bring in a little more than the last, but travel books on unexplored and unknown places in far-off lands were not particularly popular.

Everyone appeared to be absorbed with the Social world and the love affairs of the Prince of Wales.

Although she did not say so, Neisa thought that if her father would write a novel in which the hero had a title, he would have a far better chance of it being a success.

Unfortunately he could only write about the African tribes and weird religions practised in Oriental countries.

Soon after Carol's letter arrived at the Vicarage, her father told Neisa that he had to travel to London.

"There is a meeting at Lambeth Palace which I am forced to attend, and this is the chance, my dearest, for you to see your cousin."

Neisa was thrilled at the idea.

There was, however, no time to write and tell Carol that she was coming.

She and her father set off the following morning in the ancient and dilapidated gig he drove around the parish in.

It took them three hours to reach London.

Then because he was in a hurry, he deposited Neisa outside the house in Park Lane and drove off.

He did not think of explaining to his daughter what she should do if Carol was not at home – he merely told her that he would pick her up at five o'clock or perhaps later.

*

Neisa was now waiting in the exquisitely furnished sitting room.

She was sending up a little prayer that Carol would be pleased to see her cousin again as she did not want to be an encumbrance in the house until her father collected her.

The door opened and the butler asked her,

"Will you come this way please, miss?"

She walked into the hall and the butler went ahead of her up the stairs.

The house provided exactly the sort of background she expected Clive Waverton to boast of as he was so rich.

She was wishing her mother was with her to tell her who had painted the pictures and the date of the furniture.

Lady Elizabeth had been bought up in an old house and she had been a visitor at all the neighbouring houses, most of which were even older than her father's.

She therefore knew a great deal about furniture and pictures and she had taught her daughter all she knew.

When they had the chance, even when Neisa was

small, her mother had taken her to museums and made her learn how her ancestors had lived.

"You must have really missed all this," Neisa asked her once, "when you married Papa and we stayed in such strange foreign places?"

Her mother had laughed.

"I enjoyed every moment of it! Equally I want you to have good taste and to understand what is historically correct, as that is the way your grandfather's family would always expect to live."

Neisa and the butler by now had reached the top of the staircase.

He walked down a wide passage and knocked at a door.

A voice called out,

"Come in!"

He opened the door and announced regally,

"Miss Neisa Moore, Miss Carol."

Carol was sitting on a four-poster bed, half dressed.

She jumped up when she saw Neisa and ran to her.

"Neisa!" she exclaimed. "How wonderful to see you! I didn't know you were coming to London."

"I didn't know myself until last night. Papa has an urgent meeting at Lambeth Palace today and we left very early this morning. There was no time to let you know."

"All that matters is that you are here, Neisa, let me look at you. It is two years since we last saw each other and we have both grown up."

Neisa was looking at Carol, thinking she was even lovelier than she had been when she was younger.

She was aware that her long fair hair was arranged in accordance with the latest fashion and she was wearing a pale blue negligee, lavishly trimmed with lace.

It perfectly matched her eyes and accentuated the translucence of her pale and white skin.

"You look so lovely, Carol, really lovely."

"That is what everybody tells me but I don't believe a word of it."

"Why ever not?" enquired Neisa.

"Because they flatter and make a fuss of me only because I am rich and that is why I am already fed up with London and want to go back to America."

"Oh no, Carol! How can you ever say that when you have only just arrived? It is so fantastic to see you!"

"It is fantastic to see you too," sighed Carol. "At least we can be frank with each other about ourselves. You are not interested in me just for what I have in my pockets, but what I have in my brain."

She spoke bitterly and Neisa said in a soft voice,

"You must tell me all about it, but here is a small present I bought you. I meant to keep it for your birthday, but it has come into bloom and, as I was coming to London with Papa, I brought it with me."

She held out the potted plant and Carol took it.

"It is delicious," she cried. "Thank you, dearest. I would much rather be given this beautiful plant than all the jewels in Tiffany's!"

Neisa laughed.

"Well, I am not likely to go there, but it's not like you to talk in that bitter way. What has upset you?"

Carol walked across the room to a large sofa.

"Come and sit down," she suggested, "and before you do so, take off that ugly hat! I want to look at you and see if you are still as exquisite as you used to be with your glorious auburn curls."

Neisa obeyed and agreed with her about the hat, but it was the only one she could keep firmly on her head when she was driving beside her father – there was no question of buying another one.

"There, that's a great deal better and you are indeed even lovelier than I could possibly remember. I expect, as you have come such a long way, you would like something to eat and drink."

"A cup of coffee would be lovely."

Carol rang a bell.

When the maid came almost instantly, she gave the order for coffee and something to eat.

The maid vanished quickly and Carol threw herself down on the sofa.

She was looking critically at Neisa without her hat and her driving cape.

Her dress was very plain and almost threadbare in places, but it revealed her small waist and her very elegant figure.

"Are you looking forward to my ball which I told you about in my letter?" asked Carol.

There was a short silence before Neisa replied,

"Of course I would love to come, but it may not be possible."

"What can you mean – *not possible*? I am expecting you and your father to stay here with us."

"I do know how much he would enjoy it. It is just that – "

"Just what, Neisa?"

"I really have – nothing – to wear."

Carol gave a little cry.

"Oh, Neisa, how could I have been so selfish and so

thoughtless not to remember how poor you are. Of course *all* my clothes are yours – anything you want. I should have thought of it before."

She gave an exclamation as a rebuke to herself.

"I have thrown away so many things I did not want. I never for a moment thought of sending them to you."

"Well, I can assure you I should be very grateful for small mercies, because things have been so difficult lately. But Papa will have a new book coming out soon and I am praying that it will be a big success."

"And you are struggling on at the Vicarage, looking after your father and not enjoying any of the lovely things you ought to be enjoying. Oh, Neisa, do please forgive me for being so idiotic! I am very sorry."

"You are not to worry yourself, Carol. After all we live in different worlds, and I manage more or less all right in mine."

"That is not good enough, Neisa, and as we have always been about the same size, I am going to dress you as you ought to be dressed and you shall have the prettiest dress in London to wear at my ball!"

Neisa's eyes were shining.

"It is so kind of you," she enthused. "I have never forgotten how you shared almost everything with me when we were last together, which now seems a long time ago."

"I only wish I could change places with you," Carol said, "because I am fed up to the teeth with being myself."

The tone in her voice and the expression in her eyes that Neisa had not understood were back again.

She put out her hand.

"What is wrong, Carol? Tell me! You have always confided in me when we had the chance."

"It is quite simple. It is money. You don't know

13

what it is like, Neisa, to realise that the only thing people are interested in is not who you are, but what you possess."

"I am sure that is not true," protested Neisa.

Carol hesitated for a moment, then she carried on,

"I will tell you happened last night."

"What happened?"

"There is a young man whom I have seen a number of times since we came to London, who I thought was very attractive. He certainly said the most fascinating things to me and paid me greater compliments than I have ever had before."

She sighed.

"I began to feel that I was really falling in love with him and it was difficult not to believe he really loved me."

"And then what happened?"

"Last night we were at a dinner party and later we started dancing and then more young gentlemen arrived which made us for the moment rather short of girls. I was dancing with another man instead of Harry. I found him rather a bore, so I left him before the dance ended and went to look for the man I really wanted to be with."

"And then – ?" enquired Neisa, feeling sure it had been something dramatic.

"He was in the room with one other man, and they were having a drink. I was about to go through the door to join them when I heard the other man say,

'What happened to Anthea, old boy? I thought last time I saw you that you were very keen on each other.'

'We were,' said Harry. 'But when it is a question of money, there is only one direction one can take.'

The other man gave a quiet laugh.

'I understand, Harry, and good luck to you if you bring it off.'

"That is what I heard, Neisa, now are you surprised that I hate my money and wish I was like you?"

"I am sorry that you should have been so upset by what you heard, but not all men are the same, and you are so pretty that the right man will love you for yourself and not for what you possess."

"Do you really think anyone could see me except through a golden haze?" Carol asked bitterly. "No, Neisa, money will always come first. After what happened last night, I shall never believe anything a man says to me, as I will always think that he is looking at my cheque book and not at me."

"But you cannot go through life like that!" Neisa exclaimed. "It is ridiculous, – *absurd*! Of course, darling Carol, you will fall in love as your father fell in love with your mother and she with him."

"It only happens once in a thousand years," Carol said scornfully. "Papa did not marry Mama for money and she would not have cared if he had been as poor as your father."

She gave a little sigh.

"If I loved a man it would not matter to me if he had not a penny in the world. But men are different – they want money, money and more money! If a girl has it with a face like a rhinoceros, it would not worry them!"

There were tears in Carol's eyes.

She rose from the sofa to open a drawer and find a handkerchief.

"I was making a fool of myself," she said in a low voice. "But Harry was so persuasive that I believed him."

Neisa knew there was little she could do.

She only thought it was very cruel that anyone as sweet and kind as Carol should become so disillusioned.

"I am so sorry, dearest Carol, but not all men are the same and you must remember most girls would give their right hand to change places with you."

"I only wish they could!"

Then she gave a little cry.

"I have an idea!"

She spoke in a completely different voice and Neisa asked,

"What is it?"

"I received this letter this morning. It is here by my bed. Let me read it to you."

She picked up the letter and sat down on the sofa next to her cousin.

"I was not very interested when it arrived, but now I think it may help me in a way I did not anticipate."

"What does the letter say?"

"It is from the Marquis of Denholme and there is a very impressive crest on his writing paper. It comes from Denholme Park in Kent."

Neisa was listening intently as Carol read out,

"*My dear Miss Waverton.*

I have just arrived home from New York where I met your father, who told me that he had bought a house in London for you for the Season and that you would hold a ball next month and I have accepted his invitation to be present.

I would therefore much like to return his hospitality and I wondered if by any chance you were free this Friday to come to stay here for the weekend at my house in Kent.

I was having a party anyway and my aunt, Lady Sarah Holme, will be acting as my hostess and chaperone.

It would give me very great pleasure if you would

join my house party on Friday at luncheon time and stay until Monday.

We have a parade organised in the afternoon of the horses that will compete in my steeplechase which takes place on Saturday.

I expect that most of my guests will be strangers to you and I would be delighted if you would like to bring a friend with you. I think at the moment we will have more gentlemen than ladies in the party.

I am much hoping you will accept my invitation.

With best wishes

Sheldon Denholme."

Carol finished reading it and Neisa exclaimed,

"It sounds a very nice invitation and, of course, you must accept."

"You see, he says that I shall not know anyone in the party, which means that his friends are not the same as those who have entertained me since Papa and I came to London."

"It will help you forget Harry," counselled Neisa.

"What I am thinking of is something very different, and I can only do what I want to do if you will help me."

Neisa looked surprised.

"Of course I will do anything to help you if I can."

She could not imagine what it could be.

But she was feeling extremely worried about Carol. It seemed wrong for her to be so bitter and cynical.

How could that stupid young man she called Harry have possibly allowed her to overhear him saying anything so unkind and so unpleasant?

Although they were the same age, Neisa had lived such a very different life to Carol.

17

She had always felt that she must protect and look after her rather than the other way round.

If Carol's dear mother and hers had been alive, they would have made her see that she must not be so sensitive about being rich.

She must learn to recognise those men who were running after her for her money and distinguish them from those who genuinely found her attractive and delightful.

"What I am suggesting," Carol said rather slowly as if she was still thinking it out, "is that we *change places*!"

Neisa stared at her.

"What on earth do you mean?"

"Exactly what I say! You will take my place and while we are staying at Denholme Park, you will be Carol Waverton. I will be Neisa Moore, the pretty girl who has no money and nothing to recommend her except herself!"

"You must be crazy!" exclaimed Neisa. "How can we possibly do that?"

"Why ever not? The Marquis has written that I will not know anyone in his party which must mean that he has consulted some of them and they have all said they have never met me."

She paused before she continued,

"There is no reason at all why they should. After all as you must know people in London move in their own particular circle and, as I have only just arrived, I have only met the friends of Lady Margrave."

"Who is she?"

"A Peeress engaged at great expense by Papa to be my chaperone."

Neisa had vaguely heard that chaperones could be engaged for the Season for *debutantes*, who were due to be presented at Buckingham Palace and invited to all the more prestigious Social balls.

Members of the aristocracy who were poor, but at the same time had the *entré* to parties given by the most influential hostesses were more than willing to undertake this service.

Mr. Waverton had a brilliant brain for organisation and was successful in everything he touched.

Neisa was sure that he would have chosen someone most suitable socially for the post of chaperone for Carol.

"Surely, Carol, if you are going to stay with the Marquis, Lady Margrave will have to go too."

"Not if we are chaperoned, as he says, by his aunt, Lady Sarah Holme. I think Lady Margrave will find more late nights rather exhausting and will be quite prepared to have a rest if I am away."

"But how can I possibly do what you want me to?" Neisa persisted. "To begin with I am quite certain I would look wrong and everyone would immediately be suspicious that I was playing a part."

"Now you are talking such nonsense, Neisa. As it happens you are much prettier, or as Papa would say, more *gorgeous* than I am. It is just that you are wearing those shoddy clothes, your hair is out of fashion and you need a touch of powder on your nose."

Neisa giggled.

"I have always thought that that would be deemed improper in a *debutante*."

"You would be surprised what goes on in the ladies cloakrooms," replied Carol. "And of course you must have my best and most beautiful gowns to wear."

"One thing is quite certain, Carol, you cannot wear mine or they will instantly send you to the servants' hall!"

Carol laughed.

"I was not thinking of being quite so different from you as that. But I have some plainer gowns and, if not, we have time to buy them."

"Wait! Wait!" cried Neisa. "I have not said yet that I will do it. I am frightened in case I should make a mess of it."

Equally she could not help thinking that it would be very exciting to stay at Denholme Park and to take part in one of the fashionable house parties she had read about so often in the Court Circular.

She had never dreamt she would ever attend one.

"The more I think about it," Carol was saying, "the more I think it will not only be amusing but will give me a chance to know what gentlemen say when they are not so engrossed with money."

"I think you are making too much of that subject."

"You wait, Neisa, and when you hear someone you have just met saying how very beautiful you are and how thrilled he is to meet you and that he will not sleep tonight unless you promise to see him tomorrow, you can be sure he is not thinking of you – but of the thousands of pounds you have in your bank!"

"I just cannot believe every man is as bad as that," insisted Neisa.

"Well, we are going to try it out and you shall see for yourself if I am telling you the truth – "

Carol then jumped up from the sofa and ran to the dressing table.

"And I am going to be the demure, quiet, simple little country girl, who knows nothing about London and fortune-hunters reaching out with their greedy little hands!"

"Just supposing," added Neisa, "I fall in love with

one of these gentlemen. What do I say when he asks me to marry him, which I do not believe for a second he will?"

"You wait and see, you will find he disappears in a twinkling when you tell him it is all a mistake and you are not the heiress he thought you were."

"I feel certain the idea is much too complicated and something we should not do – "

But Neisa she did not speak very positively.

She knew as Carol laughed that she was intrigued and it would certainly be a change from her own life.

Once the weekend was over, it would be something to look back on and laugh about.

"You are not going to let me down, are you?" Carol demanded.

Now Neisa knew she was really worried in case she refused.

"I promised to help you if I could and if you are certain this is what you want, then, dearest Carol, I will do my best. But you must not be angry if I fail!"

CHAPTER TWO

Next the two girls sat down and composed a letter to the Marquis.

Carol made Neisa write it out on her very expensive printed writing paper.

"My Dear Marquis,

How very kind of you to invite me to your house party at the end of this week. I would love to come and I am sure Papa would want me to see your beautiful house.

I thought I would bring with me my cousin, Neisa Moore, who I am sure you will like.

She has a very dull life. Her father is the Vicar of Little Meadowfield and because he writes books they do little entertaining. In fact I am anxious for her to meet and make friends with people her own age.

We will arrive as you suggest in time for luncheon and Neisa and I are both looking forward to meeting you and seeing your magnificent horses.

With all best wishes

Yours sincerely,"

"Now you can sign it," Carol said to Neisa, "but of course with my name. I am not likely to write letters while I am there, but I might have to sign for something and if the handwriting is different, they might be suspicious."

Neisa gave a little shiver.

She was feeling sure that all this deception would end in trouble if not tears.

However, as it was amusing Carol, she did not say so – she merely signed Carol's name on the letter.

Then Carol suggested,

"As there is not much time we are going shopping."

"Shopping! What for?"

"For one thing some very pretty dresses for you. It would be a mistake for you to wear anything that did not fit you exactly and become you."

"But I thought I would wear your clothes, Carol."

"You can take my clothes as well, but I am quite determined, dearest, that you shall have some things which are specially yours and will give you, if nothing else, loads of confidence."

She gave a little laugh before she added,

"And, of course, as the Vicar's daughter I must not be overdressed and that means an array of new and simple clothes for me!"

Once again Neisa protested, but she did not persist because the scheme was making Carol so happy.

Carol ordered a carriage brought round and a smart fourgon arrived almost immediately, drawn by two horses.

Neisa was interested in them and Carol told her,

"When Papa undertakes something he never does it by halves. He has kindly not only provided me with this magnificent house from which to make my debut, but has also filled the mews. I know you love horses so when we have time, we will go and look at them."

There was certainly no time that day.

They roamed endlessly from shop to shop in Bond Street until Neisa found her head whirling.

Carol was very determined that she should have the prettiest and most striking gowns available and anything unusual she refused to buy.

However, in just a few hours they had bought what Neisa considered was a whole trousseau for herself.

And several new dresses for Carol.

"You shall have them all when you go back to the Vicarage," said Carol, "because if I wear them as myself, I think those who admire me would be disappointed."

"You would look so lovely in them all, but I cannot think why they should also want you dressed up."

"They will want their money's worth, or rather *my* money's worth," Carol responded bitterly.

Neisa now realised by the time they returned to the house that Carol was really disillusioned by the men who were pursuing her for her fortune and most especially by the young man she had overheard.

She wondered how any man who called himself a gentleman could be so blatant about his designs.

He might at least have pretended to himself that he was not pursuing Carol entirely for her money.

She was so beautiful and when she was not feeling upset, vivacious and captivating.

It seemed extraordinary to Neisa that money should matter so much.

They had only been back at the house in Park Lane about ten minutes when the Vicar arrived.

He was shown into the drawing room where they were having tea and Carol rose to kiss him.

"It is so lovely to see you, Uncle Patrick, and Neisa has been telling me what a brilliant book you are writing at the moment."

"I do hope you will enjoy it," he replied, "but I am afraid not many people are interested in the Far East."

Neisa poured him out some tea and he sat down at the table saying,

"I hope you will have time, Carol, while you are in England to come and visit us."

As he spoke Neisa was thinking how uncomfortable Carol would find the Vicarage – and how difficult it would be to entertain her.

"I would love to, Uncle Patrick, but at the moment I want you to lend me Neisa."

The Vicar raised his eyebrows and Carol explained,

"I have been asked for the weekend to stay with a friend of Papa's, the Marquis of Denholme, and to bring a friend with me. I thought it would be lovely for Neisa to see his house, which I am told is very impressive, and also his horses."

"I have heard of the Marquis," said the Vicar. "He has, in fact, some excellent horses and did very well on the turf last season."

"So you will let Neisa come with me?"

"Of course, and it is very kind of you. I am afraid Neisa does not have the chance of attending balls and all the entertainments that she should be enjoying in London, but as you are well aware we cannot afford it."

Carol smiled at him.

"Maybe your book will be a big best-seller and then Neisa can be a *debutante* in the same way as I am."

The Vicar chuckled, but both girls knew he thought this was very unlikely.

Then as if he had just thought of it, he proposed,

"I think Neisa had better stay with you until Friday. It will not be worth her coming home for just two days and perhaps you could lend her some clothes – "

He was being practical as he always had to be.

"Don't worry at all. Neisa can wear my clothes. It

is very lucky that we are the same size and it would be an unnecessary expense to send her things to London."

The Vicar looked relieved.

Neisa felt a little guilty when she remembered how many gowns Carol had bought for her, but at the same time it was a new excitement she had not expected and she was very grateful.

"Now I must be getting home," the Vicar said as he drank his cup of tea. "It takes three hours and I have just remembered that the choirmaster is coming to see me this evening."

"I have an uncomfortable feeling, Papa, that he is going to tell you the choir must have new surplices. When I looked at them on Sunday I realised most of them were in rags. I was aware that Mr. Weston was thinking the same as I was."

"It is something which we certainly cannot afford at present. In fact there are quite a number of items we need to provide before we can think of new surplices."

"I will give them to you," offered Carol. "I was wondering what you would like for a gift, and I feel, Uncle Patrick, that you would rather have surplices than a pretty piece of *objet d'art*!"

The Vicar laughed as if he could not help it.

"That is certainly true, but I cannot allow you to do anything for us when you have not even seen the Church."

"Well, when I do come and see it, I would rather it looked presentable than in rags. So do stop being proud, Uncle Patrick – buy your surplices and send me the bill. It will only be one of the many that I am expected to pay at the end of each week!"

The Vicar was slightly embarrassed, but at the same time grateful.

Neisa knew how much he disliked anything shoddy around him especially in his Church.

"I think, Papa," she suggested, to make it easier for him, "you must accept Carol's kind gift, because actually she is planning something most interesting and unusual, and if it succeeds, it will be her thank-offering."

"In that case, Carol, my dear, I can hardly refuse. But thank you, thank you very much indeed, and may what you are planning be the success you want it to be."

"I sincerely hope so too," responded Carol.

The Vicar rose.

"I must leave you, and you are quite certain that it will not be a bother to have Neisa to stay with you without her belongings?"

"I am thrilled to have her and she can quite easily have everything she needs here."

The two girls walked to the front door with him and kissed him goodbye.

He climbed into the rather disreputable old gig that was waiting outside.

As he drove off, Carol murmured,

"What I ought to give him is a really smart chaise. How can we let him drive all the way home in that rickety old buggy which looks as if it might fall to pieces at any moment!"

"I think it is good for you to see how the poor live," replied Neisa. "When you compare Papa's gig with your smart carriage we drove in this afternoon, you will not be so contemptuous of your money, but will realise just how useful it can be."

Carol laughed.

"I love you when you preach to me. I know you are thinking I am ungrateful, but just wait until you hear how everyone will talk to you when you are pretending to be me in a quite different voice from the one they would use to you now."

"I still do not believe you, Carol."

"Well, you will, and I, for the first time in my life, will hear people speaking to me in an ordinary voice and behaving in an ordinary way."

Neisa did not reply.

"Now let's both go upstairs," Carol suggested, "and make ourselves comfortable. You realise that, although you are in London, we cannot go to any parties tonight or tomorrow just in case we meet people who we might meet again at the Marquis's."

Neisa looked puzzled and Carol explained,

"If they saw you as *you*, they would think it very strange when later they are told you are *me*."

Neisa laughed.

"Now I understand and it was very stupid of me not to grasp it. But if you want to go to a party, Carol dear, I shall be perfectly happy in this lovely house."

"I would much rather be with you, Neisa, than at one of those parties where the young men are counting up how many millions I own."

"I refuse to believe all men are that dreadful."

"Well, you will be surprised at how money changes what would appear to be the most charming and delightful gentleman into the grabber and grasper of every pound he can get his greedy fingers on!"

Neisa did not answer her, as she thought that it was a great mistake to go on talking about money.

Instead she turned the conversation to the past and things they had enjoyed when they were children.

They retired to bed early and the next day Carol insisted that they went shopping once again.

Although Neisa protested, she could not help being thrilled.

Carol bought them both the most entrancing hats that the vendeuse said had just arrived from Paris.

Also they had both forgotten that Neisa would need new shoes which were smart, fashionable and high-heeled.

They had luncheon alone because, as had happened last night, Lady Margrave was suffering from a cold and a headache – she had sent a message to say that she intended to stay in bed.

"You do not know what a relief it is to be without her," Carol told Neisa. "She can only talk about the smart people she knows and is determined to procure a Duke for me before the Season is over!"

"Have you ever met a Duke?" enquired Neisa.

Carol shook her head.

"They do not seem to be as impoverished as other gentlemen and therefore they are not hanging around me."

"And would you like to be a Duchess?"

"Not particularly, but it would please my Papa, who wants me, as you know, to move in the same Society as Mama did before he spirited her away to America."

"Not in the same manner that my father had spirited away her sister."

"Now that was really romantic," agreed Carol. "I only wish someone would fall in love with me in the same way."

She spoke wistfully and Neisa remarked,

"I am certain that you will find someone who will.

But you do realise that my mother lived a very strange and unusual life and, although she never complained, much of it was very uncomfortable."

"Did she mind?"

"She was so much in love with Papa that, if they had told her she had to live on the pavement like some of the Indians do, I believe she would have accepted it quite happily just because she was with him."

"That is what I want," asserted Carol. "You do not understand, Neisa. I want to love someone who loves me and who is not in the least interested that I am rich enough to buy him anything he wants."

Neisa put out her hand and laid it on Carol's arm.

"I am sure, dearest, you will find a man like that. It upsets me to see you so disillusioned and so bitter. Try to accept things as they are and leave the future in the hands of God."

"I don't suppose that God is particularly interested in the complaints of a girl who is too rich. We all know He is concerned with the poor, the needy and – "

"And those who seek love," interrupted Neisa. "As you have just said, love does *not* depend on money."

"I do agree with you. At the same time you do not really understand what I am feeling, but you will after this weekend. Anyway, if nothing else, we will enjoy seeing the Marquis's horses and if I tell Papa about them, he will want to buy some which are even better."

"Which you will enjoy," said Neisa softly. "It can be very frustrating when one is longing for a ride, but has nothing on four legs to accommodate one!"

Carol laughed and then she kissed Neisa.

"You are trying to make me ashamed of myself for continually complaining. Well, I am determined to make you eat your words on Monday when you come back from the Marquis's and you find that the young gentlemen who paid you so much attention will have disappeared."

"Do you mean to say," Neisa replied horror-struck, "that we are going to tell them we have deceived them?"

"No, of course not – but out of sight, out of mind. When you are no longer there, they will look for another heiress who is more available!"

They went to bed early again that night after they had laughed, talked and argued with each other.

Neisa realised that Carol had not minded that she had been invited to three different parties, which, because she was with her, she had refused.

She begged her to go, but Carol said she was sick of parties and she only hoped that her father would let her go back to America soon.

"There are so many rich people in America," she explained, "that no one takes any particular notice of me. Also, as you know, Society there is not confined to just one set of people who are born into a certain position."

"I always understood it embraces everyone who can afford it," replied Neisa, "which does mean we are back to money!"

"I suppose that is true of the First Avenue set, but Papa seems to know everyone from the top to the bottom and I think that is much more fun."

Neisa did not say anything more.

She was well aware that Mr. Waverton wanted his daughter to marry into the best Society available.

Carol was making plans so that no one could ruin the deception they intended to play on the Marquis's party.

"I am sending the carriage straight back to London as soon as it has dropped us at Denholme Park," she told Neisa, "and I will tell them to come back for us very late on

Sunday night so that we can leave early on Monday if we want to. I do not want the coachmen to have a chance to gossip with the other servants."

"I had forgotten that they might give us away."

"Papa always says if you want something done you have to think of every top, bottom and side of it, and that is what I am trying to do where our charade is concerned."

"That is just the right word for it," smiled Neisa, "or perhaps *drama* would be a better word."

"Let us hope that it does not turn into one!"

The girls kissed each other good night.

Neisa found it difficult to go to sleep as she was so excited at what would happen tomorrow.

Although she knew her father would think Carol's plan was wrong, she wanted to make Carol happy.

If this really amused her, why should she complain?

*

The maids had already packed all their delightful new dresses into smart trunks.

Neisa knew that she had to remember that the one with Carol's initials on was the trunk she must have in her bedroom.

When she was dressed in the travelling gown Carol had bought for her and wearing the hat to go with it, she looked in the mirror and found it hard to recognise herself.

The only person who had to be let into their secret was Carol's lady's maid.

Hannah had been with her for five years and she trusted her completely.

Hannah was, as it so happened, an Englishwoman, who had gone out to America to marry an American who changed his mind at the last moment.

He abandoned her in New York with no money and it was just at that moment that Carol wanted a new lady's maid as hers had left her to be married. She had engaged Hannah on an impulse because she was English.

It was something she never regretted, as Hannah came from the old school of English servants, who were utterly and completely loyal to whoever employed them.

She looked after Carol as if she was a very precious child who could not look after herself.

When she was told the secret of what the two girls were planning, she giggled,

"Well, that's something new at any rate. If you asks me, Miss Carol, it'll make your father laugh when he hears about it."

"We are much more frightened he might be angry," said Neisa.

"The Master's got a sense of humour. He knows as we all do that Miss Carol, pretty though she be, is run after for her money. I sees the world from another angle and it's a good thing too!"

"I thought you would understand, Hannah, and it will be fun for Miss Neisa to think that she is rich instead of having to count the pennies as she does at home."

"You're both as pretty as pictures," chirped Hanna, "and if the gentlemen we're to meet don't think so, then they must be as blind as bats!"

"I have the feeling," came in Neisa, "that we shall be playing second fiddle to the horses. I was looking at the sporting page of *The Times* yesterday and there was a long description of the Marquis's new racehorses. One of them has just won the big race at Newmarket."

"Very well, we will just have to compete with the horses," Carol cried, "and if no one gives us a second look, then we will know exactly where we stand!"

They both laughed at the idea.

They drove away in a smart carriage with Hannah following them with their luggage in a brake.

Neisa felt it would be difficult for anyone to ignore either Carol or herself.

As far as she was concerned, her new clothes had transformed her – from what could be described as a plain little sparrow into a Bird of Paradise!

She boasted a string of pearls round her neck which were worth thousands of pounds and two pretty bracelets round her wrists were set with real stones.

Carol had supervised every garment she put on and her hair had been cut and arranged by a top hairdresser.

Hannah had noted everything he did, making quite certain she could repeat it when they arrived at Denholme Park.

If Neisa was looking fantastic, Carol was playing her part very cleverly.

Her dress was much plainer than Neisa's and yet it was well cut and accentuated her perfect figure.

The little hat she wore was exceedingly becoming, although it was much plainer than the one she had chosen for Neisa, but it still had a chic and elegance which only the French could provide.

"You don't look to me much like a poverty-stricken Vicar's daughter," commented Neisa with a chuckle.

"We need not make him quite as poor as he actually is. I can always say if anyone asks questions, I have a rich relative who is kind to me."

"I only hope no one will ask me questions," Neisa sighed, "because I am certain to give the wrong answers and get into a muddle."

"They will not ask you any questions," Carol said

scornfully. "They know only too well that if you dressed yourself in diamonds from head to foot, you could well afford it."

Now she was bitter again and Neisa remarked,

"I think you must keep to your part and say sweet, kind and gentle things about everyone, however unpleasant you think they actually are."

Carol laughed.

"That's true. Papa has always said a man who is a good actor believes every word he is saying. That is why he is suspicious of men in business who are too glib."

"That is something you must not be," replied Neisa.

They both laughed.

It was only as they were approaching Denholme Park that Neisa started to become nervous.

Because she had never been to any grand parties, she felt she might do the wrong thing and upset Carol.

However, she had never felt shy in the slightest in meeting strangers, having travelled to so many divergent parts of the world with her father.

She had talked with Potentates and Arab leaders as well as chatting with weird characters who lived in caves or mountains.

She wanted to play her part successfully for Carol's sake and was only afraid that she might let her down by not being familiar with the Social world.

As they drove up the drive she was entranced with her first sight of the large and imposing house.

The sunshine was glittering on the windows and the Marquis's standard was flying proudly on the roof.

It did not seem real, but something out of a dream.

They crossed an ancient bridge spanning the lake

and as they did so, a flight of white doves flew round the side of the house and settled on the green lawn that sloped down to the water.

The scene was so beautiful that Neisa caught her breath and felt it was a special omen that everything would go right for Carol.

The carriage drew up outside the front door.

As a footman ran down the red carpet, Carol said in a whisper,

"You climb out first and remember you are *me*."

Neisa did as she was told.

She walked up the steps to the front door followed by Carol.

Four footmen were in attendance and a butler who bowed respectfully.

"I think you must be Miss Waverton," he began. "His Lordship is expecting you."

He walked ahead and threw open a door to a room at the end of the hall.

As he did so, he announced in a stentorian voice,

"Miss Waverton and Miss Moore, my Lord."

The room seemed to Neisa to swim in front of her and then she saw there were a number of people standing by the fireplace.

One man detached himself and came towards them.

She assumed that this was the Marquis, although he was not in any way what she had expected.

She had known from what she had read about him that he was an aristocrat of considerable consequence.

She had not expected him to be so good-looking or, in a way she could not explain, authoritative.

She had also assumed, because he was a friend of Carol's father, that he would be much older.

As the Marquis reached her, he held out his hand.

"I am very delighted to welcome you to Denholme Park, Miss Waverton, and I only wish your father could be with you."

"It is most kind of you to have me," Neisa managed to reply. "And may I introduce my cousin, Neisa Moore."

The Marquis shook hands with Carol and turned to introduce them both to his friends.

They were all gentlemen with the exception of his aunt, Lady Sarah Holme.

"I am so pleased you could come," Lady Sarah said to Neisa. "I was so afraid at one time that we would be a bachelor party, and I would have to stay upstairs and not be allowed to dine with them. But now you have arrived and there are several other ladies joining us tomorrow."

The gentlemen, who were all young and charming, clustered around Neisa.

But there was one who she thought seemed a little different from the others.

She was not certain why until he shook her hand.

Then she had a feeling of revulsion which she could not explain – it was something she very seldom felt about anyone and when she did, she always learned later that her intuition had been right.

This person was in some way or another up to no good and unpleasant.

However, there was no question of talking to any particular gentleman.

They all appeared to be speaking at once and, not surprisingly, discussing horses.

"You know, of course," one of them said to Neisa, "that after luncheon we are to have a parade of the horses that will be competing in the steeplechase tomorrow."

"The Marquis did mention it in his letter to me," answered Neisa.

"It is a tradition in the family," he continued, "that all our horses and his should be paraded today. Therefore anyone who wishes to change his mount before the actual race can do so."

"I call that a very sensible idea."

"You will not be surprised to learn," he confided, "that the Marquis's horses are usually better than anything we can breed. Therefore, if he does offer me a chance of riding one of his, I am only too pleased to accept."

He lowered his voice as he added,

"I have always suspected that those competing in the race bring their worst animal, so as to make sure they have a good excuse for being provided with another by the Marquis and so have a better chance of winning!"

Neisa laughed.

"I think it is rather clever of them."

"I am sure that your father owns the best horses it is possible to find anywhere," the young man persisted.

"He certainly has several in America that are very fine," responded Neisa.

"That is just what I expected, and I daresay when he comes over here he will buy the cream of the bunch at Tattersall's, which are far too expensive for anyone like myself!"

There was a note of envy in the young man's voice that Neisa did not miss.

She thought it was just the sort of conversation that would upset Carol.

She glanced at her cousin.

Carol was now talking to a young gentleman who

looked charming and was obviously anxious for her to hear what he had to say.

The Marquis offered Neisa a glass of champagne and as she thought it was what Carol would have done, she accepted it.

"I hope," he said, "that you are going to enjoy my steeplechase tomorrow. And may I say that after you have viewed the horses, if you want to bet on which will be the winner, we have a special bookie just for my house guests, and a quarter of anything he gains goes to charity."

Neisa was impressed.

"That is very good of you, my Lord."

"I think that it is something we should do and also it prevents any ill-feeling amongst those who cannot afford to gamble."

The Marquis moved away as he finished speaking and Neisa thought that at least was one point in his favour.

Everything she had already heard about the dashing young blades of the Social world had not been particularly complimentary.

Her father deprecated gossip, but it was impossible, even in the village of Little Meadowfield, for people not to talk.

They somehow learnt about the love affairs of the Prince of Wales and a number of distinguished aristocrats.

Even Betsy, the woman from the village who came to clean the Vicarage, would say,

"Them goin's-on in London would have shocked me mother and there's no use in sayin' it wouldn't!"

It was inevitable that someone would bring back stories of 'goings-on' in high places.

Many local young girls would find it impossible to obtain employment in Little Meadowfield, so they would travel to London seeking positions in service in one of the grand houses where apparently there were big parties every night with distinguished visitors and even Royalty.

When they returned home or if they were capable of writing, they would tell their parents and anyone else who wanted to listen what they had seen and heard.

As far as Neisa could make out, there were endless *affairs de coeurs* between titled gentlemen and beautiful ladies.

It had all meant very little to her.

Yet she could not help thinking that undoubtedly the Marquis of Denholme with his title, his horses and his money would be a focus of attention.

The ladies who arrived later were very smart and certainly not *debutantes*.

They had a sophistication about them which Neisa had anticipated and the reality at Denholme Park, however, was even more intriguing for them than she had imagined.

Their delight at being a guest of the Marquis was very evident.

They looked at him with appealing eyes and talked in soft seductive voices as if they were addressing someone they loved.

By the time they went into luncheon, Neisa could not help thinking that she and Carol were not in tune with the rest of the party.

The Marquis announced to his guests that because luncheon was an informal meal, he was not going to place everyone as he would do at dinner.

"I just want you to sit with whomever you like," he said, "and tonight I will choose you partners whom I think you ought to like!"

They all laughed.

Two of the ladies who had just arrived, as soon as they entered the dining room, sat down on either side of the Marquis's chair.

Lady Sarah took the end of the table.

Neisa found herself sitting halfway down the table with Carol in much the same position on the other side.

The two gentlemen on either side of Neisa made it very clear that they thought her money could buy her the very best horses available and they hoped one day that they would have a chance of riding them.

They were somewhat naïve about it and not, she thought, particularly tactful.

She managed, by talking about horses she had seen abroad and letting them lecture her on English breeds, to get through luncheon without much difficulty.

The ladies left the dining room first.

It was then that the gentleman she had considered rather unpleasant addressed her as she passed by him,

"I would like to talk with you, Miss Waverton, and I will make sure that tonight I will have a chance to do so."

She smiled at him as she thought it polite.

When she walked outside the dining room door, she found she was standing beside Lady Sarah.

"Who is that gentleman," she asked, "who spoke to me just now? I was introduced to him, but I did not hear his name clearly."

"That is a cousin of my nephew's," replied Lady Sarah. "His name is Randolph Holme, and he is, I might say, something of a problem."

Neisa wondered in what way.

There was, however, no chance of a conversation with Lady Sarah as the other ladies were all talking to her, asking questions about what would happen that evening.

"I am quite sure," one said, "that the Marquis has something up his sleeve that will be very exciting for all of us. I only hope I will be smart enough to compete with the millionaires!"

"You always look smart, Lady Georgina," replied Lady Sarah, "and I do think you will find that my nephew does not expect you to do anything spectacular this evening as he did the last time you were here."

"That's a major relief!" exclaimed Lady Georgina, "except that it was such fun and so unusual last time. I just cannot believe that tonight will only be an ordinary feast of eating and drinking!"

Lady Sarah chuckled.

"It will not be as bad as all that. At least you will not have to act out a charade this time."

Neisa wondered what had happened last time and thought, although she did not like to ask questions, it must have been intriguing.

Carol joined her and she asked her in a low voice,

"What do we do now?"

"As soon as the gentlemen join us, we will go out to look at the horses and bet on which one will win the steeplechase."

"I cannot afford to do that," whispered Neisa.

"Don't forget that you are *me*," Carol muttered in a voice she could hardly hear. "You must put at least twenty pounds on anything you fancy."

"Twenty pounds!" Neisa exclaimed in horror.

"A quarter goes to charity and they will think I am mean if I give less than that amount."

"Yes – of course, I had forgotten I am *you*."

She could not help ruminating that twenty pounds would feed her and her father for almost two months.

It seemed seriously appalling to risk so much on a single horse.

Almost immediately, because the Marquis wanted them to move, the gentlemen joined the ladies.

When they walked out through the front door, they could see the horses already coming from the stables.

They were the finest horses Neisa had ever seen.

There were several outstanding stallions as well as one or two mares she thought looked very swift and were probably good jumpers.

In her life she had ridden such an odd assortment of animals from donkeys and mules to blue-blooded Arabs.

This made her conclude that she might be a better judge in some ways than those who had ridden nothing but the best British thoroughbreds.

Each horse was led out by a groom and they were bridled but not saddled.

The Marquis and his guests stood on the steps and the horses were paraded round and round in a circle.

Then they were lined up, each well apart from the others, so that they could be closely inspected and those who were interested could talk to the grooms holding them.

Neisa went from one to the other, patting the horses and looking at their feet and height.

There was one stallion which she considered really overwhelmingly outstanding and she was not that surprised when she was told his name was Champion.

He was to be ridden in the steeplechase only by the Marquis, as he was his favourite mount.

"I am sure that Champion will win," she said to the groom who was holding him."

"I shall be extremely disappointed if he does not," a voice came from behind her.

She spun round and it was the Marquis.

"He is the most beautiful stallion I have ever seen," enthused Neisa.

"And I am quite sure, Miss Waverton, that you are a good judge of horseflesh."

She was a little uncertain if he was being sarcastic or genuine and so she replied,

"Horses like Champion are only bred occasionally, and often where one least expects it. I think you are very lucky to own him, my Lord."

"I think so too, but it is no use betting on Champion because even if I ride him round the course and win, I am disqualified as being the owner of the steeplechase."

Neisa laughed.

"That's a very funny reason!"

"It is a very fair one as I have the advantage of the steeplechase being on my land, so I know it well, and also, as you have just said, I have the best horse."

"But surely you will ride in the race, my Lord?"

"Of course," he replied, "but just for the pleasure of showing Champion off, which I can assure you he enjoys very much indeed."

"As he has every right to."

She patted Champion again and then she remarked,

"I would really love more than anything else to ride a horse like Champion, so that I can compare him with any other horse I have been privileged to ride."

She knew as she spoke that the Marquis looked at her in surprise.

"That is something no one has ever dared to ask me before, because they would be certain I would refuse!"

"I was really talking to myself rather than to you,

my Lord. Of course I should not presume to ride anything so wonderful."

She paused for a moment.

"My cousin did say that there might be a chance we could ride tomorrow before the race starts."

"If that is what you would like to do," the Marquis replied, "then anything in my stable, except Champion, is at your disposal."

Neisa's eyes lit up.

"That would be very exciting for me!"

The Marquis gave a somewhat wry smile.

"Do you really mean that or are you being polite? After all I am sure that your father owns the finest stable in Colorado or wherever it is you live in America."

"That is exactly what he likes to think," said Neisa after a moment's thought, "but anyone who travels a great deal knows that where the horses are concerned, as with people, one is continually being surprised. They turn up in the most unexpected places, and if one is lucky, one has a chance of riding them."

"I know what you are saying, Miss Waverton, but I make it a rule that I and I alone ride Champion, and I am afraid that on this occasion you are going to be unlucky."

Neisa did not explain to him that she was really not thinking at that moment of Champion.

She was remembering a stallion she and her father had discovered in a strange place in the East where it had arrived by a circuitous and unusual route from Syria.

It had been bought by Arabs, ridden by Arabs and finally sold by Arabs.

They had managed to buy it very cheaply and it had been the finest horse she or her father had ever mounted.

When they came back to England they had left him behind, but it had been with a man they could trust to look after him and love him until he died.

Neisa had often found herself thinking of that horse at night and she wished over and over again that he had not been left behind.

She realised the Marquis had misunderstood what she was saying – yet she thought it would take too long to explain, so she therefore advised him,

"You must be extremely careful of Champion, my Lord. If anything happened to him, I am sure you would never be able to replace him either in your stable or in your heart."

The Marquis looked at her quizzically.

"You are quite right and I promise you I will take the greatest care."

He then moved away and Neisa continued with her examination of the horses.

Finally, because she knew it was expected of her, she chose another horse – it was nowhere near Champion in quality, but still a fine animal.

As she did so, Randolph Holme came up to her.

"Are you putting your thousands on Mercury?" he enquired sardonically.

"Not thousands of pounds," replied Neisa. "But I think he is a very fine horse."

"I saw you admiring Champion."

"He is in a different category altogether and I can understand why the Marquis keeps him for himself."

"As he keeps very many others things," mumbled Randolph. "He is not in the least over-generous to his poor relations, I can assure you."

The way he spoke was unpleasant and niggling.

Neisa considered it extremely bad form on his part to disparage the Marquis who was, after all, their host.

She therefore moved on without speaking.

"Now you can have anything in the world, Miss Waverton," he continued, as he walked beside her. "What is it you want that you will not be happy until you find it?"

Neisa felt he had an ulterior motive in his question and she was not certain what it was.

Lightly, because she did not like the look of him, she replied,

"Of course, I am looking for another Champion."

"And if you find one?"

"I think it would be impossible, but one can always keep on trying, and I am quite certain that my father would be interested in finding one for me."

"And you, what might you be offering in return for achieving your greatest wish?"

Neisa did not answer and after a moment, he said,

"You are very beautiful. I am quite certain that any man would climb up the Himalayas to pick you a flower if that is what you would desire, or dive down to the bottom of the sea to bring you back a perfect pearl."

Neisa felt he was even more obnoxious than when she first shook hands with him.

She responded in a voice which she meant to sound cold and somewhat repressive,

"As none of these things are likely to happen, there is no point in discussing them."

Actually, because it came naturally to her, Neisa's voice was always soft and sweet.

But when she looked up at Randolph, she thought that the expression in his eyes was extremely menacing.

47

"What then," he added, "can I offer you, except my deepest admiration which comes from my heart."

Neisa turned her head away.

Then to her relief she saw the Marquis was telling the grooms to lead the horses round in a circle once again.

She moved away from Randolph saying,

"Oh, now we can examine the horses a little more closely."

She walked over to the side of the courtyard as she spoke, but Randolph joined her.

"Even when you are doing your best to snub me," he breathed in a voice that only she could hear, "I still find you utterly adorable – in fact *irresistible*!"

CHAPTER THREE

When the horses were taken away the party went in for tea.

It was served in the drawing room and there was a lavish provision of cakes, scones and chocolate biscuits.

Neisa thought that it was a spread she would like to produce at home for her father.

Carol, who had been watching the horses in a rather detached manner, was sitting a little outside the circle.

A young gentleman who she had been told was Sir Peter Jackson joined her.

"I can see," he commented wryly, as he sat down, "that you are not as ecstatic over horses as your cousin."

"I enjoy riding very much," replied Carol, "but I am not obsessed by it."

"Quite right, Miss Moore. I have another interest too and I find it difficult to think of anything else."

Carol thought he was talking more to himself than he was to her.

She asked curiously,

"What is your interest, Sir Peter?"

"Do you really want to know about it?" he asked, "or are you just being polite?"

"I am just curious – " Carol responded with a smile.

"Very well, I will tell you."

He moved a little nearer to Carol so that he did not have to raise his voice.

"Two days here are going to be very trying for me, because I can hardly wait until Monday – "

The way he spoke to her was so intense that Carol became really interested.

"Do tell me all about it, Sir Peter."

"I have invented a brand new mechanical system of controlling a ship or yacht, and it is being very carefully considered by the Admiralty at this precise moment."

There was a noticeable and distinct hint of triumph in his voice, but the expression in his eyes told Carol just how anxious he really was feeling.

It was clearly a problem for him to behave normally when there was so much at stake.

"It is very clever of you, Sir Peter, and I suppose, if the Admiralty accept, you will be looking for someone for finance."

It had passed through her mind to wonder if he had guessed she was not whom she pretended to be and hoped that she would assist him.

"Certainly not," he replied sharply. "It is my own invention and I intend to develop it myself!"

He spoke so positively that Carol looked at him in surprise.

"Why do you feel so strongly?" she enquired.

"Because," he replied, "there are so many people in this world scrounging off those who are rich and making no effort to finance anything for themselves."

Carol was intrigued.

"You really intend that if the Admiralty does accept your invention, you would finance it all yourself from your own resources and run a Company that is entirely yours?"

"I am surprised you know so much about it, but that is exactly what I propose doing."

"Supposing you fail?"

"If I do, it will be my own fault, and my invention cannot be as perfect as I believe it to be. So I will just have to go back to square one and start again."

"I think that is very brave and sensible of you!"

Sir Peter smiled.

"If there is one thing that I would dislike more than anything else, it would be to be financed by my wife. You must be aware that the men buzzing round your cousin are like bees around a honeypot!"

Carol laughed.

"That is very true, but I assure you my cousin does not encourage them."

"They need no encouraging," exclaimed Sir Peter scornfully. "If they can grab some money into their hands without earning it through the sweat of their brow, that is exactly what they desire and I despise them all for it."

"Equally if you are risking everything you possess on your one invention, it may, if things go wrong, cripple you for the future."

"If so, it will be my own loss and no one else's. I would not have to apologise to those who have trusted and believed in me when I have lost their money."

As Carol found this conversation so interesting, she could not help asking him,

"But why do you feel like this? Why are you more determined to go your own way than almost any other man would be?"

Sir Peter was silent for a moment.

"I suppose I like being independent, and if I marry,

which I have no intention of doing at the moment, I will be Master in my own house and my wife will depend on me."

He gave a little laugh that had no humour in it.

"Look at all those men clustered round your cousin simply because they have been told how tremendously rich her father is. Can you imagine how any decent husband would feel when he is reminded day after day that it is *her* money they are spending and not *his*?"

"I think that is a little unfair. I am sure my cousin would never say anything so unkind."

"If she did not say it, she would think it, and that is something I would find completely unendurable!"

Carol was quiet, as there did not seem any more to be said.

Then feeling that she was sympathetic to him, Sir Peter continued talking.

He told her how he had always been fascinated by ships when he was a little boy and how gradually the idea of a new way of directing them had come to his mind.

"I expect you would call it imagination, but I often feel as if someone from the past, perhaps a sailor who had never been given a chance to express himself, was guiding me with my designs."

"I am certain that sort of thing can happen," Carol agreed, "but I still think it very brave of you to go it alone."

"I shall know the best or the worst on Monday and, as you can imagine, it is so hard for me at the moment to concentrate on anything else."

"All I can do is to wish you the very best of luck, Sir Peter," Carol murmured quietly.

"I do believe you mean it, Miss Moore, and if you pray, as I know you do, because your father is a Parson, please pray that my invention will be accepted, because I know that I have done a really good job."

"Of course I will pray for you, Sir Peter."

It was the very first time that anyone had asked her to pray for them and she was rather touched.

Sir Peter was good-looking and at the same time he had that alert, intelligent look which she had seen in other men who were as successful as her father.

Like him they had fought their own way from the bottom to the top of the ladder.

On an impulse she added,

"Shall I be prophetic and say that just as you use your instinct, I am now using mine. I know that because you are you, that your invention will be accepted and prove to be a great success."

Sir Peter stared at her.

It was almost as if he was seeing her for the first time.

"Thank you for saying so, Miss Moore, and I really do believe you mean it."

"I mean it with all my heart and I am sure – as this has happened to me several times in the past – that what I am saying will come true."

Sir Peter smiled at her and as she smiled back, she felt that he was the nicest gentleman she had ever met – he was so totally different from those who had pursued her in London.

Sir Peter, thinking that after what she had just said, Carol was particularly interested in ships, took her to the picture gallery, where there were many pictures of ancient ships and several which had been painted recently.

"This is not Sheldon's collection," he explained to Carol, "but his father's. The late Marquis was completely fascinated by anything that could sail on water."

"So I can see," remarked Carol.

"Sheldon has always been a good friend of mine," Sir Peter continued, "and when I used to stay here as a little boy, his father explained to me how ships had developed over the ages, and then took me sailing on his yacht round the North coast of Scotland."

"So he inspired you?"

"Indeed he did, and please understand that if this invention of mine succeeds, it will be due to his influence when I was six and first came to Denholme Park."

They admired the other pictures in the gallery until it was time to dress for dinner.

When Carol went upstairs she found Neisa in a very grand bedroom on the main corridor running from the State staircase.

"My goodness, Neisa!" she exclaimed. "They are really doing you proud. This is a room fit for a Queen!"

Neisa laughed.

"You realise it was meant for you. And now can I take a look at your room?"

They walked down the corridor to find that Carol had been allocated a room four doors away from Neisa.

It was a nice comfortable room with a large bed.

Equally, as Carol had realised, it was not nearly as grand as the one which had been intended for her as 'the heiress.'

"Sir Peter is right," she cried. "People should not make such a fuss about money."

Neisa looked surprised.

"Was it Sir Peter you were with?" she asked. "You were away a long time."

"He was telling me how much he despises men who

run after money, and how he would never marry a woman who owned more possessions than he did."

"That must have been a change for you to hear."

"It was and I found it very intriguing. At the same time I am well aware that he will drop me like a hot brick when he learns who I am!"

Neisa looked at her sharply.

She thought it would be ironic if Carol fell in love with a man who refused to marry her because she was rich.

Carol, however, did not say any more.

She merely chose a pretty but rather demure gown to wear to dinner.

She said she would come to Neisa's room before going downstairs. She was determined to make certain she looked the part she had to play.

"So far it hasn't been all that frightening," smiled Neisa, "except that I don't like that relation of our host."

"You mean Randolph Holme. I gather from some remarks I heard about him that he is always hanging about the Marquis asking for money."

"Does the Marquis give it to him?"

"I believe so," replied Carol, "because he is the heir presumptive."

"Then I hope he never comes into the title. There is something rather creepy about him and I only hope I don't have to sit next to him at dinner."

Her hope, however, was not granted.

*

By the evening the party had grown so that when they walked into dinner, they sat down thirty in the dining room.

Randolph was at Neisa's side and she was a little surprised to find herself on the left of her host.

The Marquis had seated an attractive Viscountess on his right.

Neisa mused that, if nothing else, they were treating Carol as if she was of considerable importance.

'It is something she should be enjoying,' she told herself, 'rather than remain so cynical as she believes it is only about her money.'

She thought herself that it was because the Marquis was very grateful to Mr. Waverton and therefore wished to make a fuss of his daughter.

As far as Carol was concerned she was delighted to find herself sitting next to Sir Peter Jackson.

They could carry on from where their conversation had left off when it was time to dress for dinner.

"I wanted to sit next to you," Sir Peter began, "so our host kindly rearranged the table so that we could be together."

"I think you only wanted that because I am a good listener," Carol teased him.

"You are also very lovely, very charming and most intelligent, and that is an unusual threesome where many women are concerned!"

Carol laughed.

Then once again they were talking about subjects that interested them both.

And to Sir Peter's surprise he found that there were a great number, most of which he had never discussed with a lady before.

At the top of the table Neisa asked the Marquis,

"Do tell me all about your beautiful house. When I came up the drive, I thought at first it must have been built by the Adam brothers, but when I saw the balconies I was afraid I might be mistaken."

The Marquis smiled.

"No, you are quite right. The house was originally constructed by my ancestors in the reign of Charles II. In the 1750s the Adam brothers built on a new façade and added the East and West wings."

"I felt it was their work, but why the balconies?"

"They were added, as you might guess, during the Regency, when balconies became fashionable, as you can see all too clearly at Brighton."

"Of course, I remember reading there was quite a craze for them in those days."

"They were a fad at the time. A number of friends have suggested I remove them. But I like them, as they have always been there since I was a child, and to me they are an integral part of my ancestral home."

"Of course you are quite right to keep them. Now please tell me about some of your pictures and furniture."

The Marquis looked surprised – this was not the sort of conversation he would expect to hold with a lady.

The majority of his female guests were always far more interested in him than in the provenance of his house.

He was astonished that Neisa knew so much about architecture and the arts.

They talked animatedly until Randolph on the other side of Neisa, chirped up plaintively,

"I am being neglected. I think it extremely unkind of my cousin, who has so much, to demand more of you than I am getting!"

Neisa laughed.

"It was I who was asking him a great number of questions which he was kind enough to answer for me."

"You can ask *me* any questions you like," Randolph persisted, "but it is easier for me to tell you how lovely you are and how impossible it is to be so near to you without my heart beating tumultuously. I want above anything else to *kiss* you."

Neisa felt shocked at his familiarity, especially over the dinner table and then she remembered that he believed he was speaking to Carol.

She became convinced that he was only interested in Carol's money and that he was merely working up to the moment when he would propose marriage to her.

It made her feel uncomfortable and as soon as she could politely do so she turned again to the Marquis.

They talked about his fabulous horses.

She longed to tell him of the Arab stallions she had ridden in Syria and the small but very fast horses that had carried her and her father in India.

But because that was impossible, she managed to make the Marquis tell her about the many places he had visited and of the many horses he had ridden in other parts of the world.

In fact the time seemed to slip by very quickly in his company.

Almost before Neisa realised it, Lady Sarah was rising from the far end of the table to take the ladies away.

"How are you enjoying yourself?" Carol whispered to Neisa.

"I am having such a wonderful time and thank you, dearest Carol, for bringing me here. It is all like a fairy story. I am only scared it will all vanish like a dream and I shall suddenly find myself back at the Vicarage wondering what I should cook Papa for dinner!"

Carol laughed.

"I will not let you wake up too soon, Neisa, and I know tomorrow you will be thrilled by the steeplechase."

"I only wish I could ride in it."

"I would not like you to do so," answered Carol. "I am told it is quite dangerous. Last year one of the riders broke his leg and his horse fell so badly that it had to be put down."

Neisa drew in her breath.

"I hope it doesn't happen tomorrow. It would upset me too much."

"I think the Marquis will take every precaution to see it does not."

The gentlemen appeared rather more quickly than was usual from the dining room.

Carol moved across the room towards Sir Peter and there was an expression of eagerness in her eyes as she did so.

It made Neisa wonder again what would happen if Carol really did fall in love with Sir Peter, who had said quite categorically he would not marry a woman who was richer than he was.

Then she heard the unpleasant voice of Randolph Holme behind her.

"Why are you looking worried, my beautiful one? There should not be anything troubling you at this moment when everyone wants you to be happy."

"I am happy, but unfortunately one cannot always be flying towards the stars. There must be moments when one is left behind on the ground without wings!"

She was talking to herself rather than to Randolph.

However the Marquis overheard and he interrupted,

"Have I overlooked something in providing elegant entertainment for my guests, Miss Waverton? Is it possible that I should have given them all wings?"

Neisa giggled.

"That is what we all long for, but luckily we can fly in our dreams and in our imagination."

"That is just what I always attempt to do," mused the Marquis. "But sometimes things misfire and one has to accept the bad with the good."

"And for some of us it is always *bad*," Randolph grumbled in a disagreeable voice.

The Marquis did not comment, but walked away just when Neisa wanted him to stay.

"Why do you have to upset your cousin?" she asked Randolph. "You know that he is trying to help everyone to enjoy themselves and that sort of remark is *very* unkind."

"There is no reason why I should be kind to him for he is not kind to me. But I can always be compensated by *you* being kind to me and I can assure you that I need your kindness desperately."

Neisa had an uncomfortable premonition that at any moment he was going to ask her for money.

So she rose from the chair she had been sitting on and walked towards the Marquis.

He was talking to Lady Sarah and when she joined him, they both looked up at her as if wondering why she was interrupting.

"I was just wondering," began Neisa, "as I see you have a grand piano at the end of the drawing room whether you would like me to play quietly as a background to the conversation. I promise you it will not be a performance."

The Marquis smiled at her.

"I can think of nothing nicer, Miss Waverton."

"I might have thought of that myself!" Lady Sarah exclaimed. "There is a woman in the village who plays the organ in Church and is very good on the piano too."

"I think that we shall be far more content with Miss

Waverton and as she has so kindly offered to play for our benefit, I accept the suggestion with gratitude."

He walked to the piano with Neisa.

As she sat down on the piano stool, she suggested,

"I think that for this party some light music would be correct. I may be wrong, but I feel that you would enjoy something more classical."

"You are so right, Miss Waverton, and I shall make you play it for me another time."

Neisa smiled at him.

He thought what a very sweet face she had, lovely long auburn hair and sparkling blue eyes – despite the fact that her clothes were just a little over flamboyant and for a young girl she was wearing too much jewellery.

Carol, to make sure that people knew the difference between them, had insisted that Neisa wear her mother's pearls and a diamond bracelet on each wrist.

Carol was putting her jewellery into a flamboyant box when she found two small but very valuable diamond earrings.

"These are wrong for a *debutante*," she remarked. "At the same time, as I have so much money, I expect that I would have wanted to bedeck myself."

They were certainly very becoming, but Neisa had a feeling her mother would not have let her wear them.

Looking at her intently the Marquis was thinking it would be impossible for any girl to look so very lovely, so young, so perfectly innocent and, although it was a strange word, *untouched*.

Yet how was that possible when, as he had heard, she was being pursued by every man in London.

According to the gossip she had already received a dozen proposals of marriage.

'She must be extremely sophisticated,' he now told himself, 'equally she is clever enough to disguise it.'

Neisa was softly playing some catchy tunes which had become popular in Vienna, some of them waltzes.

She thought it would be nice if there were people dancing.

Randolph was now leaning on the piano and as if he could read her thoughts, suggested,

"I would love to dance with you, Miss Waverton, and I am told that tomorrow night my cousin has engaged a small band for us to dance in the ballroom."

"That will indeed be delightful."

"Not for you, as you have attended dozens of balls and danced with dozens of gentlemen. But when I dance with you, it will be different. I want more than I can say to hold you closely in my arms – "

Neisa considered he was becoming embarrassing.

She played a little louder so that she could not hear what he was saying.

She was pleased when Lady Sarah announced that as they would have a long and busy day tomorrow, she felt that everyone should go to bed early.

"That includes the gentlemen," she stressed. "You are not to drink too much, because you will need all your wits about you when you see the new fences Sheldon has erected specially for tomorrow's steeplechase."

There was a murmur around the room and some of the gentlemen were wondering if they had made a mistake in deciding to ride their own horses instead of borrowing one of their host's.

Finally they all retired to bed.

As Neisa was moving towards the door, Randolph Holme was beside her.

"You are being most elusive," he complained, "in leaving me so early. But I will tell you later how much I mind being separated from you."

Neisa did not answer.

As she walked slowly upstairs she wondered what he meant.

Because she was in one of the first bedrooms on the corridor, Lady Sarah bade her goodnight and so did several of the other ladies, who were sleeping, Neisa gathered, on the other side of the corridor.

At the far end was what Hannah told her later was the Master Suite.

"How do you know?" Neisa asked as Hannah undid her gown.

"His Lordship's valet tells me that you're in one of the rooms which is usually reserved for Royalty. As his Lordship don't like too many guests near to him, the rest of the party are on the corridor leading in the other direction from the stairs and the gentlemen'll be in the East Wing."

Neisa was not particularly interested, but she was glad, however, that Carol was only four rooms away.

'If I am frightened in the night,' she thought, 'I can easily go and sleep with Carol.'

Hannah hung up Neisa's dress in the wardrobe and then left her to undress herself.

"I'll call you in the morning, miss – "

"At eight o'clock, please. Breakfast is at half-past and the steeplechase starts at ten o'clock."

"I knows that, miss, and a nice fuss there is about it too. You'd think it's the end of the world instead of just a horse race!"

As Hannah left the room Neisa remembered to lock the door.

It was something her father had always made her do when they were staying in an unfamiliar hotel or with some strange people in the East.

She noticed, however, as she turned the key that the lock was old. It was actually made of silver and not very substantial.

'It must have been there when the house was first altered by the Adam brothers,' she pondered.

She climbed into bed and then she began to think of the curious remark Randolph Holme had made to her.

Was it possible that he was thinking of coming to her room?

She just could not believe he would dare to do so!

Yet there were many stories of improper behaviour amongst those who moved in London Society.

Two people who were having an *affaire de coeur* would be given adjacent rooms if they were staying in the same house party.

Neisa was indeed very innocent, as the Marquis had deduced.

But she was also too intelligent not to be aware that such things could and did happen.

Carol had related to her some of the gossip about people she had met with Lady Margrave.

Neisa thought such scandal should not have been told to Carol.

Now, as she thought about it, she was frightened.

Suppose Randolph, who she now actively disliked, tried to enter her room?

She had locked the door, but he was tall and broad shouldered.

She doubted whether, if he used all his strength, the door would be strong enough to withstand him.

Because she felt so unsettled at such a possibility, she decided to go at once to Carol's room and so jumped out of bed.

She put on the very pretty dressing-gown Carol had bought her – it was the colour of her eyes and trimmed with real Valenciennes lace – and there was a pair of dainty blue slippers to go with it.

Neisa stood thinking about what she should do.

If she went out through the door into the passage, she might be seen by someone who would think it odd – or worse still, she could run into Randolph coming from his room to hers.

'I could not bear that,' she decided.

She crossed the room to the window.

It was long and low like all the windows built by the Adam brothers and when the balconies were added, the windows had not been altered.

It was very possible to step onto the balcony by just raising the window as far as it would go and one only had to stoop a little to climb out.

Neisa did just that.

Then she found, as she had expected, the balconies did not fully link with each other.

Any other girl would have been terrified at the idea of leaping from one balcony to another – there was a drop of over forty feet between them.

Neisa had climbed up parts of the Himalayas and mountains in Turkey with her father and mother without damaging herself.

Therefore she found no difficulty in jumping across to the next balcony.

Actually there was no one sleeping in the next room and the curtains were drawn.

She hoped there was no one outside in the garden below to see her.

She jumped again and passed another room and as she reached the third room, she heard voices from inside.

She stiffened.

It was with great difficulty that she forced back a loud exclamation as she realised that the man speaking was Randolph Holme!

She would have recognised that rather unpleasant, smarmy voice anywhere.

Then to her sheer astonishment, she realised that he was speaking in Arabic.

"Now do exactly as I tell you," he was saying. "Go now while it is still dark and fasten the wire onto the fence. Don't forget it is the fifth one we jump after having left the starting-post. I am sure there will be no one about at this time of night."

"I'll do so, Master," the other man replied again in Arabic.

"Be certain you can easily pull the wire taut and be careful not to do so until the Marquis's horse has actually taken off for the jump."

There was a pause.

It was as if Randolph wanted to make sure that the man had fully understood all his instructions.

"As I have told you already, as soon as the horse falls and the Marquis is thrown onto the ground beside it, push the little pill I have given you into his mouth before anyone can see what you are doing. He will be *dead* in just a few seconds."

The stark note of triumph in Randolph's voice was unmistakable.

Neisa drew in her breath.

"Now do you understand?" he finished.

"I understand Master. I'll carry out my Master's orders and nothing will go wrong."

"That is just what I hope and trust. And when his Lordship is dead you will have the money I promised you. It will be doubled when I marry the rich young woman I am going to visit now."

"I understand, Master, and I obey your commands."

From the way he spoke Neisa was sure that the man was a Berber and was now bowing to Randolph.

She then realised with a horror that seemed to pulse throughout her whole body what Randolph was plotting – it was 'the accidental death' of his cousin, the Marquis, so that he would inherit the title.

And he would obtain all the money he needed from her, because he intended to seduce her.

It all flashed through her mind like lightning.

Only her self-control prevented her from crying out in terror.

She had to find help at once.

She must save the Marquis from certain death when the wire pulled up on the fence would cause Champion to fall.

It was a dastardly plot.

A plot which only a man as despicable as Randolph could plan.

Turning round, Neisa started to retrace her steps.

Moving from balcony to balcony, she reached her own room and then she paused outside the window.

She knew that it would be a mistake to go into the passage.

She must reach the Marquis by the balconies.

Quickly she jumped onto the balcony next to hers in the other direction.

She could only pray that when she did manage to find the Marquis, he would believe her.

He might think she was inventing an incredible tale which had no foundation in fact.

The next two balconies were easy.

Then as she leapt onto the last balcony on the main building, she knew it led to the Marquis's room.

It was a different shape to the others – longer and a little wider.

She was afraid the Marquis might not have opened his window and if she knocked on the glass to attract his attention, someone else might hear her.

It was only that she was terrified as she had never been terrified in her life.

If Randolph did force an entry into her room and found she was not in bed, he might then look for her on the balcony.

She had left her window wide open at the bottom. If she had just wanted some cool air, she would most likely have opened it at the top.

All these imaginings passed through her mind.

Her heart was beating furiously.

She was petrified that something would prevent her from reaching the Marquis in time to warn him.

Then tomorrow morning he would ride to his death at the fifth jump in the steeplechase.

She clambered panting onto his balcony and caught the lace of her dressing-gown on one of the elaborate stone flowers with which the balcony was ornamented.

She released herself by tearing it a little, thinking it

was a pity to spoil anything so pretty, something she would never have again.

Then she looked at the window and saw with relief it was wide open at the bottom.

She did not hesitate.

She felt just as if Randolph was running after her to prevent her from spoiling his infamous plan being put into action.

Without thinking further she scrambled through the open window and stumbled noisily onto the floor.

As she raised herself to her feet, she could see the Marquis staring at her in sheer astonishment.

He was lying in a magnificent gold four-poster bed draped with crimson velvet curtains.

As Neisa now straightened herself, he exclaimed in a horrified voice,

"Miss Waverton, *whatever* are you doing here?"

Neisa walked towards his bed.

"I have – come here to – warn you," she mumbled and her voice was somewhat unsteady, "that both you and – Champion are in – d-deadly d-danger."

The Marquis stared at her.

"Danger! What do you mean?"

There was a distinctly sharp note in his voice and it made Neisa feel as if she had been caught doing something wrong.

She put out her hands as if to hold onto something and felt herself sway.

Her eyes flickered and then she closed them.

The Marquis quickly thought she was about to faint and suggested thoughtfully,

"There is a chair just behind you. Do sit down."

Neisa obeyed him.

Then she lifted her hands to rest them for a moment over her eyes – she was trying to make herself concentrate on what she must do.

"Now please tell me," the Marquis resumed in a calm voice, "what has upset you and why you have come here to me."

"There is a plot to make – Champion fall and when you are thrown – you will be given – a p-poisonous drug."

The words came out jerkily from between her lips.

She was aware that the Marquis was looking at her as if he did not believe her and she was imagining what she was saying or perhaps playing some trick on him.

Then he saw how pale she was, the frightened look in her eyes and the trembling of her hands.

Very quietly he soothed her,

"There is no hurry. You are quite safe now, so tell me everything from the very beginning."

"That is – just what I want to do, and I am sorry – to seem so stupid – it was just such a s-shock."

"What was a shock?"

"Overhearing Mr. Randolph Holme – planning it all with a man who I think is – a Berber."

The Marquis made a little movement with his hand before he asked,

"Were they speaking in English?"

"No, – in Arabic."

"You speak Arabic?"

The Marquis's voice sounded incredulous.

Neisa thought he must now be quite certain she was inventing the whole tale – perhaps to attract his attention or because she was a little mad.

"Yes, I – can speak Arabic and, as I have been to North Africa, I am – certain the m-man was – a Berber."

"I have already seen the man in question," said the Marquis, "and I learnt from members of my staff that he did not speak any other language except his own."

"Mr. Holme was telling him exactly what he should – do."

"And I suppose you were outside the window?"

Neisa nodded.

"I was going – to my cousin's b-bedroom along the balconies, since I did not – want to go down the corridor."

"Why not?"

The question was almost like a pistol shot.

For a moment Neisa could not answer it.

Then as she realised the Marquis was waiting, she stuttered hesitatingly,

"Mr. Randolph Holme had said something strange to me downstairs and I was afraid – d-desperately afraid he might come to my room."

"Why did you not lock your door?"

"I did," answered Neisa, "but the latch – seemed a little frail and I – thought he might try to force it – open."

She thought as she spoke how much the Marquis must despise her for being so inadequate and pathetic.

But there was nothing she could do, but to tell him the whole truth.

"So you thought you would go to your cousin along the balconies, and you were not scared of climbing from one balcony to another at such a height?"

"I have climbed mountains – and worse – places."

Her voice died away and the Marquis asked,

"Then you heard what was being said through the open window?"

Neisa nodded.

"Now tell me exactly what Randolph was saying."

"He – said that the Berber was to go now and – fix a wire on jump number five – and when you approached it tomorrow – he was to wait until – Champion had actually taken off for the jump, before he pulled it up – *tight*."

Her voice deepened as she went on,

"Champion would fall – and you would be thrown and doubtless – be unconscious. Then he was – to push a poisoned pill into your mouth before anyone else appeared and you would be dead – in a few seconds."

There was a silence until the Marquis asked her,

"So you realised at once, after you had overheard this conversation, that you must come to me at once?"

"I – had to save you and Champion! How could I allow anything so horrible and wicked to happen and – not try and prevent it."

She looked up at the Marquis almost as if she was willing him to answer her.

He said quietly and deliberately,

"It was very brave and resourceful of you. Now I want you to go back to bed. Say nothing to anyone and try to sleep."

Neisa clasped her fingers together.

"You have to prevent it happening? You *must* stop the Berber! He will now be on his way to fix the wire on the fence!"

The Marquis shook his head.

"You must be intelligent enough to understand that I have to catch them red-handed. If I accuse them of what you have told me, they will merely say you are hysterical and then they will strike another time when I have no idea what they indeed to do."

"Oh – no! They cannot do that!" cried Neisa.

"Then you must do as I say. Go to bed at once and I will take you to a room where you can sleep without fear and by a less dangerous route than the balconies!"

He climbed out of his four-poster bed and picked up a long dark robe that was lying over a chair.

He was wearing a silk nightshirt, but it completely covered him.

Neisa looked away shyly, the blood rising into her pale cheeks.

As the Marquis put on his robe he looked at her and smiled.

"Now I am decent, so don't feel embarrassed!"

He picked up a candle and walked across the room to where there was a door by the window.

As Neisa joined him she could see that there was a room adjacent to his bedroom, quite obviously his private boudoir.

They walked across the boudoir without speaking.

Then the Marquis opened another door, but cleverly concealed by layers of bookshelves.

As the door swung back, she saw from the light of the candle in his hand they were in a bedroom which was as magnificent as the one she had been allocated.

It passed through her mind that this was doubtless the room used by the Marchioness of Denholme whenever there was one.

"This is your bedroom tonight," he explained, "and the room beyond it is your boudoir, though I expect you will not want to explore it now. When you do, I think you will find several books that will interest you, because they are written about this house and my ancestors."

"I should enjoy reading them."

She thought he smiled at her as he was lighting the candles by the bed.

Then the Marquis pulled back the satin covers and she saw that the bed was made up.

"You will be safe here, but I will now leave the two doors between us open in case you are frightened.

"Thank you more than I can possibly say for being brave enough to come to me tonight and clever enough to understand what was being planned. There is no one else in this party who could have done that."

"And you will be careful – " Neisa urged him.

"Very careful, I promise you, and I know you are worrying about Champion."

"He is *so* magnificent, I could not bear anything to happen to him."

There was a faint twinkle in the Marquis's eyes – he thought that any other woman would be worrying about him first.

"Thank you again, Miss Waverton."

Because it seemed quite natural, he bent his head and kissed her gently on the lips.

She gave a little gasp.

Then before she could realise what was happening, the Marquis disappeared through the communicating door.

She was left alone in the bedroom.

CHAPTER FOUR

The Marquis rose as soon as dawn broke and then dressed himself quickly.

Having been in the Army at one time he was used to doing things for himself at a speed which most people could never achieve.

He ran downstairs and let himself out of the house by one of the back doors.

It was too early for there to be any servants in the passages and no one was to be seen in the garden.

The sun was just rising.

When it touched the flowers and the blossom on the trees, everything turned beautiful and enchanted.

It seemed quite unbelievable and the Marquis could hardly credit it that any of his relations would actually plan to kill him and to behave in a manner that his whole family would think appalling.

But Randolph had always been tricky and quite different from any of his other relatives.

His own father had often laughingly called him 'a changeling'.

Now, if what he had heard last night was indeed the truth, the Marquis was inclined to believe it.

How could anyone behave in such a manner who bore his name and that of his ancestors who had upheld the pride and dignity of England for centuries?

He had paid Randolph's bills over and over again.

Every time he wrote out yet another cheque he had talked to him quietly and seriously, explaining that as head of the Holme family he had a great number of relations to look after.

"You are not the only one, Randolph," he had said, "and if I give you more than your fair share, it means that someone else will go empty-handed."

He had known by the expression on his cousin's face that that aspect did not trouble him in the slightest.

Randolph had always been very selfish, greedy and jealous of him.

'Now,' the Marquis told himself, 'he has gone too far. I will have to find some way of controlling Randolph in the future – for this must never happen again.'

He walked on.

His thoughts were all concentrated on the dastardly plot that had been planned against him.

It was impossible for him to enjoy the beauty of the morning or listen to the song of the birds.

The steeplechase had always been one of his most favourite interests since he had first introduced the race.

It was a strictly private affair – only his guests and one or two of his close friends in the neighbourhood would be asked to compete.

But he did not exclude people from nearby villages coming to watch as he knew it thrilled them.

Just as it thrilled him to watch how well the horses could jump and how experienced their riders were.

He thought, because he had Champion to ride, that this steeplechase would be the best he had ever arranged.

He had been looking forward to it so eagerly and he still could not believe that it might be his last.

If it had not been for one of his guests, both he and Champion could have died at the fifth jump.

He thought again how incredibly brave it had been of the Waverton heiress and how she had come to him by climbing from balcony to balcony.

Although he rather doubted her story that Randolph would break into her room, he had to admire her courage in finding such an ingenious route when she needed to see her cousin.

It seemed strange that unlike other women he had known, she was not frightened of heights.

He had heard a great many stories about her father. No one, however, had said he was a mountain climber as his daughter had implied last night –

As he strode on, the Marquis was thinking how frail she looked – not only frail to climb mountains but also to want to ride a horse as big and powerful as Champion.

'I expect she is just showing off,' he told himself.

At the same time she appeared so quiet, gentle and sweet, which did not seem to fit in with her appearance.

When he had kissed her goodnight, it had been an expression of gratitude.

She seemed so young and petite as she stood beside him, so he thought of her more as a child than a woman.

But when his lips touched hers, he was aware of an unreal feeling within himself. Now as he thought about it, he was almost sure that she had never been kissed before.

Then he told himself this was impossible.

As he had felt at first, she is a very good actress.

Despite her success in London and the number of men who had thrown themselves at her feet, she behaved just like a very young girl – one who knew nothing of the Social world and was more at home in the country.

'She is certainly surprising,' he told himself.

The fifth jump was in a very special position and it made the steeplechase very different from any other he had ever ridden in.

He had run the course through the trees in the park and over some bare land – then between two woods and he had found an ideal place for a challenging jump.

There was a straight and fairly long run up to it and the riders could urge their horses to gallop faster than they had done so far in the race.

Then at the end of the long run there came the fifth jump, which had originally been a hedge dividing one field from another.

There were trees on each side and once the horses had taken the jump there was a short piece of level ground ahead.

As the Marquis drew nearer to the jump, he realised that if Randolph had really planned to kill him, he could not have found a better spot at which to do it.

The woods on either side were a protection against any interference and the jump could not be seen from the spectator's stand.

The hedge, on his instructions, had been allowed to grow up without being cut back.

It would be easy for a horse like Champion to take the jump in his stride even though it was one of the highest fences in the whole race.

He deliberately approached the jump through the wood just in case the Berber or anyone else was watching the fence.

But there was no one to be seen.

The rabbits rustling away in the undergrowth ahead of him and the squirrels jumping overhead assured him he was the only interloper. At the moment the wild life had the woods to themselves.

However, he was cautious enough to approach the hedge carefully.

He looked as if he was just inspecting it and not as if he was searching for anything that should not be there.

When he was close, he looked through the leaves at the top of the jump.

Now he could see the strand of thin wire that Neisa had told him he would find.

He could see it gleaming in the early sunshine.

He realised at once how dangerous it could be.

It only needed a short inspection to see what would happen.

When the Berber pulled the wire taut at the moment Champion had taken off for the jump, it would add at least a foot onto the jump.

It would be just impossible for any horse, even one as good and as strong as Champion, to clear it.

Now looking over the fence the Marquis could see that some sharp stones had been added since yesterday on to ground on the far side.

It was where the horse would fall and its rider be thrown from the saddle.

There was a grim expression on the Marquis's face and his lips were set in a hard line.

He realised that what he had been told was the truth and his cousin Randolph intended him to die.

He could see only too clearly how cleverly it had all been planned.

The Berber would emerge from the direction of the wood and approach the jump unseen from the far side of the fence.

It would be impossible for him to see that the man was there until it was too late.

Gently, so as to disturb the wire as little as possible, the Marquis with a sharp instrument cut it at the other end of the jump from where the Berber would be manipulating it.

When he pulled it, it would not rise a foot higher and taut as he intended, but merely slip towards him.

He did not cut the wire through completely – he left a small strand which would break when it was pulled and would not be apparent until the trap was set in motion.

Then, because he knew it would be a mistake to let anyone see him, he walked back into the wood.

He retraced his steps over the fields and orchards until he was in the garden.

It was still very early and there was no one to see him enter the house by the back door.

He walked upstairs to his own room and sat on his bed trying to think what he should do about Randolph.

If his cousin failed in his attempt to kill him today, there was always tomorrow!

It was impossible for him to be permanently on his guard – or for him to rely endlessly on someone like Miss Waverton to save him from destruction.

'What on earth can I do? What the devil can I do?' he asked himself over and over again.

For a moment he could not think of a solution to his appalling problem.

He was thinking again about Miss Waverton and how brave she had been.

Then he thought it would be a mistake for anyone to know she had not slept in her own room last night, and it would cause endless gossip amongst the servants if it was known she had slept in the bedroom next to his.

It was important that no one should imagine there was any particular bond between them.

The Marquis therefore waited until the clock told him it was half past six.

Then he walked through the connecting door that led into his sitting room.

The boudoir door was still half open, as he had left it.

He moved quietly into the room.

The curtains had not been drawn and the sunshine was streaming brightly into the room.

The Marquis walked to the bed and saw that Neisa was fast asleep.

Because it was hot she had pushed down the sheet and he could just see the outline of her breasts beneath her diaphanous nightgown.

Her beautiful auburn hair flowed like a torrent over her pillow and her shoulders.

She looked exquisitely lovely and it was hard for him to believe that any man had never held her in his arms.

She seemed little more than a child, lost in a fairy tale dream.

'She is so ethereally beautiful,' he mused, 'and far too perfect to be involved in anything quite so unpleasant as a murder.'

He had a sudden impulse to bend down and kiss her lips as he had done last night.

Then it had been just a simple gesture of gratitude. Now he knew that he was deeply moved by her beauty in a way that he had seldom been moved by other women.

Because it seemed almost a crime to waken her, he thought he would take a look at the door of her bedroom – as she had said that she was afraid that Randolph might burst it open in the night.

Although the Marquis felt it unlikely, he wanted to know for certain whether or not he had tried.

He quietly opened the door of Neisa's room.

The candles that had been alight beside the bed had burned down. Two of them were out altogether whilst the third had just a tiny flame still flickering.

He could see the open window where Neisa had set out to reach her cousin's room.

The Marquis then walked towards the door.

The lock seemed intact when he first glanced at it and then he realised that in a subtle way, Randolph must have managed to manipulate the key.

He had obviously been in the room, found his prey had vanished and knowing he was defeated, he had given up the chase.

The Marquis's expression was grim as he looked at the lock.

He vowed that never again would it be possible for any guest to enter a lady's room unless she opened the door herself to him.

He would instruct his carpenter to fit steel bolts to the inside of every door, so it would be impossible for any potential lover, however ardent, to force open a door once it was bolted.

Then the Marquis walked back to Neisa.

Very gently he covered her hand with his as it lay limply on the lace edged sheet.

"Please wake up," he urged. "It is time for you to be awake."

Neisa opened her eyes and for a moment she stared at the Marquis.

Then she murmured,

"I was dreaming – about *you*."

"I am very flattered, but you must now go back to your own bedroom."

For a moment Neisa did not seem to understand.

"Oh, of course! What time is it?"

"It is nearly a quarter to seven, and it is important no one should know you have slept here."

"No, of course – not."

Neisa sat up in bed.

The Marquis saw that her dressing-gown was lying on a chair, so he walked over to the window with his back to her.

She jumped out of bed and quickly put on her blue dressing-gown with its elegant lace trimming.

Her slippers were beside the chair and she slipped her feet into them.

She tidied the bed, turning the pillow over so that it did not appear that anyone had slept there.

The Marquis turned round as she was pulling back the satin cover she had taken off last night.

"That is very sensible of you," he told her quietly. "We do not want anyone talking about what has happened or making Randolph curious as to where you had gone."

"Do you – mean that he came – into my room – last night?" she stammered.

"I think so," he nodded, "but it is something which will not happen again."

He saw the fear in Neisa's eyes.

"You were safe last night, and I promise you, you will be safe tonight and any other night you stay in one of my houses."

"Thank you! Thank you for letting me sleep here,

my Lord. I would have been so terrified – if he had come to me, as I believe – he intended."

"He had *no* right to," asserted the Marquis and his voice was angry.

"But you were very kind to me and what have you done – about the jump?"

The words came slowly from between her lips.

The Marquis had the feeling that when she said she was dreaming of him, she had been saving him from death.

"All is arranged, but you have to act your part very cleverly and not make anyone think you are at all anxious about Champion and me."

"But he will be safe?"

"I promise you I will take the utmost care of him – and of myself!"

"You will not – take any risks, my Lord?"

"There will be no risk now at jump number five," the Marquis told her positively.

He saw the expression in her face and asked her as if he could not help himself.

"Does it matter so much to you?"

"Of course it does! How could I possibly want you to – die in such an appalling way or – for Champion to be injured so that he might never be the same again?"

"None of these things are going to happen. Now go back to your bed until your maid calls you. Remember you have slept peacefully and nothing unusual or unexpected has happened during the night."

"I will try to remember," she murmured obediently.

She smiled at him and walked to the open door.

As she reached it, she turned round.

"You promise, my Lord, you will be *very* careful?"

"I promise."

She smiled again at the Marquis and then hurried to her own bedroom.

It was exactly as she had left it and she blew out the last flickering candle.

As she climbed into bed she began to pray.

It was a very fervent prayer that the Marquis would be kept safe and that Champion would not be injured.

And that no one would ever know that she had been involved in anything so horrible and so cruel.

Then she began wondering again how the Marquis would be able to protect himself in the future.

If the Berber failed to raise the deadly wire at the jump, then Randolph would merely think of another way.

He was obviously determined to destroy his cousin and become the Marquis of Denholme himself.

'He must be stopped at all costs,' Neisa told herself.

But like the Marquis, she was finding it difficult to think of how he could be foiled and he certainly could not be accused of doing something which could not be proved.

Neisa lay worrying in bed until Hannah came in to call her.

*

She pulled back the curtains and brought in a tray with a small pot of tea, a cup and a slice of thin bread and butter.

"It's such a lovely day," Hannah was saying, "and they're all looking forward downstairs to the race, which of course his Lordship'll win as he always does."

"I too am hoping he will win today," replied Neisa cautiously, but she was not thinking of the race.

Hannah dressed her in one of the beautiful dresses that Carol had bought for her in Bond Street.

Neisa was about to go down to the breakfast room when Carol came bursting in.

"Let me look at you," she cried. "You have to look your best today because this is a very smart occasion."

"No one will look at me, Carol, as they will all be concentrating on the horses and how much money they are going to win!"

"I expect that's true. Money is more important to them than anything."

The bitterness was back in Carol's voice.

When they arrived at the breakfast room, Sir Peter Jackson was there and he rose to his feet as they entered.

As he did so Neisa caught the expression on Carol's face and knew that she was in love – it made her look even more attractive and lovelier than ever.

Neisa heard Sir Peter say as he went to Carol's side,

"Did you sleep well? And did you pray for me, as you promised you would?"

"Of course I did," answered Carol. "And as I told you, your invention is going to be accepted and you will feel like jumping over the moon!"

"We will jump together," smiled Sir Peter.

He pulled back a chair for Carol and brought her what she asked for from the silver dishes on the side table.

Neisa was helping herself to eggs and bacon when Randolph Holme came into the room.

He walked across to Neisa without speaking to the others and once he was beside her, he asked her in a low voice,

"Where did you sleep last night?"

It was the question she had not been expecting and for a moment she could only stare at him.

"What do you mean?"

"I came to say goodnight to you as I had promised I would and you were not there."

Neisa looked away from him.

"That was something you have no right to do and if I had not been sleeping with my cousin, I would have been very angry."

"I thought it was where you might have gone, but you knew I wanted to talk to you and to tell you how much you mean to me."

Neisa turned away.

"Today we need to be absorbed by the steeplechase, and that is more important than anything else."

"Nothing could ever be more important than you," Randolph replied. "I think you will find that what I have to say is far more interesting than watching a whole lot of sweating horses."

"That is where you are wrong," answered Neisa. "I would rather watch the horses than anything else."

"Very well, I will let you do so. But when the race is over, we will walk in the garden or, if you would prefer, sit in the conservatory."

Neisa determined that nothing would make her do either of these things, but it would be a mistake to say so now.

She thought that only Randolph could talk of such a private conversation whilst the Marquis was lying dead at the fifth jump.

'He is so ghastly, inhuman and completely without any feeling of decency,' Neisa fumed to herself angrily.

She sat down at the table to eat her breakfast as a number of the other guests came into the room.

"We have been looking at all the horses," called out one of the gentlemen, "and if you ask me they are just as excited about the race as we are!"

"Of course they are," another agreed. "I have never met a horse yet who did not enjoy a good race especially when he has a good chance of winning it!"

They all began talking at once about racing – what they felt before a race, after it, and if they won.

Whilst everyone was talking away, Neisa managed to move so that she was no longer sitting next to Randolph.

Although he looked crossly at her when he realised what she had done, he did not say anything.

Sir Peter Jackson and Carol were the only two not talking about the steeplechase and every time Neisa looked at them, she could see how interested they were in each other.

She began to worry again as to what would happen when Sir Peter learnt who Carol really was.

'I am sure that she has never felt like this about any other man,' Neisa told herself. 'And I could not bear her to break her heart over a man who will never love her.'

Yet it was difficult to think that was possible. She could see how animated and attentive Sir Peter was.

She thought that when he was talking to Carol there was a look of affection as well as admiration in his eyes.

However she could not be sure, as at this moment she could not be sure of anything –

She could not even be sure that Randolph was still planning to destroy the Marquis and Champion.

When breakfast was finished, she and Carol walked upstairs to fetch their hats.

They waited to go to the starting-post with the men and there were several brakes to take them there.

The Marquis had departed from the breakfast room sooner than anyone else and Neisa realised he was going ahead to see that everything was in order.

It was difficult for her not to beg him once again to be very careful and not to take any risks with himself or Champion.

As she watched him walk away, she thought that if anything did happen and he was mortally injured, it would be all her fault, as she would not have impressed on him strongly enough that he must take good care of himself.

She appreciated, however, that any such move on her part might attract Randolph's attention.

If he did not put his dastardly plot into operation today, he would undoubtedly keep it for another time and then there might be no one to warn the Marquis.

'Like Carol, I can only pray,' she determined.

She wished that she could tell her father what was happening as she was sure that his prayers would be more effective than anyone else's.

They all drove down to the starting-post.

When they arrived Neisa thought no one could look more magnificent than the Marquis seated upon Champion.

He was moving among the riders, giving directions and making sure that every one of his guests was mounted on the horse they wanted.

One gentleman changed his mind at the last moment, saying frankly, that his own horse was not up to scratch.

He requested one from the Marquis's stable and a groom ran to get it for him, returning with an exceedingly fine looking chestnut, which was young and frisky and, as the groom assured the rider, an excellent mount.

"I will have a bet on myself," the Marquis's friend boomed, "and now I have a good chance of winning I will make it one thousand pounds!"

Neisa gave a gasp.

She could not imagine that anyone would wish to risk such a lot of money on a single race when there was so much competition.

"Can he really afford it?" she asked Lady Sarah.

"His father is an extremely rich man," Lady Sarah replied, "and made a fortune, I am told, in shipping."

"Then I need not worry about him!"

"If you worry about all these young gentlemen you will be grey before your time," smiled Lady Sarah. "They enjoy taking risks in life and nothing any of us say can stop them."

Neisa thought she would rather they took risks with money than with life.

She had managed to avoid speaking to Randolph since leaving the breakfast room and now he was mounted on one of the Marquis's best horses.

She had to admit, although she disliked him, that he did have a good seat on a horse.

But no one could look so fine or so magnificent as the Marquis in his dark green jacket and brown top hat.

At the same time there was no doubt there was a family resemblance between the two men.

'With Randolph as the dreadful black sheep,' Neisa told herself, 'and a very creepy one.'

Perhaps because she was thinking of him, he looked towards her and then rode up to her side.

"Are you wishing me luck?" he enquired.

"In winning the race? I feel sure that your cousin will win."

She realised it was something she should not have said and yet the words came from her lips before she could prevent it.

Randolph laughed and it was not a pretty sound.

"Perhaps he will and perhaps he won't, but I have the feeling that if you are backing me, I will come in first and that is what *I* want."

Because it was impossible for her to go on speaking to him without being rude, Neisa turned away.

Randolph muttered something she could not hear as she walked to where Carol was talking to Sir Peter, who was riding quite a good-looking horse which was his own.

Neisa was sure he would dislike having to borrow one from the Marquis.

'He is a very proud man,' she decided, 'and he will never marry Carol if he learns she is so rich.'

Yet she knew by the way he was talking to her that he found her entrancing.

Carol was looking up at him with a softness in her face which Neisa had never seen before.

'Why must money matter so very much?' she asked herself angrily.

She thought it incredibly wrong that it was money which had turned Randolph into a murderer.

And money which would break Carol's heart.

The Marquis was now directing the riders into line for the start.

Seats were provided for the spectators in a very fine stand. From the top of it an onlooker could see for a long distance, in fact most of the course.

The only point that was hidden completely was the fifth jump and that was why, Neisa realised, Randolph had chosen it for his wicked act.

The Marquis now finally succeeded in putting all the horses in a line.

Next the Head Groom, acting as the official starter, held a green handkerchief in his hand.

"*One – two – three*," he counted and dropped it.

They were off.

As they all rode past the stand, Neisa felt her whole heart go with the Marquis.

He looked so very handsome on Champion that she just could not believe anything could hurt him.

Then, as she saw Randolph riding just behind him, she shivered.

It was easy to see the first and second jumps which were quite close to the stand.

Then the riders began to spread out for the third.

Binoculars were available on the stand and Neisa raised hers to see that the Marquis was leading the field as Champion took the third jump with six inches to spare.

'There is no one to beat him,' she concluded.

Then she remembered the hidden wire in the fifth jump and it was at the fifth that Champion was due to fall.

'Please God, please save them! Do not let anything happen to them!' she prayed.

Putting down the binoculars she now clenched her fingers together in her intensity.

Carol was standing a little further away and she too was watching the horses and in particular Sir Peter.

He was a good rider and was now in fourth place.

'If he wins,' Carol was thinking, 'it will be an omen that his invention will be accepted and he will be in a very good mood this evening.'

She knew they were going to dance and she wanted

to dance with Sir Peter as she had never wanted to dance with any other man.

He was extremely good-looking, but that was not the only reason as she felt when she was near him that they had an affinity together.

They seemed to think the same on many subjects and were amused by the same things.

For the moment Carol wanted to think that he was not really serious in what he had said about women having money and that he would never do anything but stand on his own feet.

More than anything she wanted to think of him as a gentleman who interested her and attracted her – he made her feel in a way she had never felt before.

It was as if something warm and wonderful went out from her body towards him and it was as if he felt the same.

'Please God let Peter win, because it will make him so happy,' Carol prayed.

She tried not to think that on Monday they were to say goodbye to Denholme Park.

Sir Peter would go to London to see the Admiralty and perhaps after that she would never see him again.

If he did see her again and learn who she was, what would he think and what would he say?

She could not bear to think about that question or how to answer it.

She only wanted to go on talking to him as they had yesterday and she hoped it was how they would talk again when the race was over.

Neisa was realising that by now the riders had taken the fourth jump and were nearing the fifth.

She prayed more desperately than ever.

She became aware that her whole body was rigidly tense.

What *was* happening?

Had the Marquis really made it safe for Champion to jump the fence?

Was he in some way going to avoid it?

Would the Berber's wait there have been wasted?

'Oh please God, please don't let there be a terrible accident!'

She closed her eyes in fervent prayer.

Then as it was impossible not to look, she lifted her binoculars.

She could only see from the stand when the horses rode towards the sixth fence.

It seemed to her almost a century had passed before the first rider came into sight round the side of the wood.

She could not see all that clearly as when she lifted her binoculars to her eyes they were misty.

But she was able to count one horse through – two – three – four –

Then as they galloped on and neared the sixth fence she saw the first horse jump.

It was Champion.

She was so relieved that for the moment she could only slump onto her seat.

She felt as if she was fainting.

Whatever might have happened at the fifth fence, the Marquis was safe and so was Champion.

Neisa was not aware that she had been holding her breath and now it came in deep gulps.

There was no need to watch the race any longer.

It was then the Viscountess who had been sitting at the Marquis's side last night at dinner came and sat beside Neisa.

"I can see our host is winning the race as is usual," she chirped, "and no one will be surprised. He always gets what he wants – he is a very lucky man."

Neisa made a little murmur as if she agreed.

"I expect like all the *debutantes*," the Viscountess went on, "you will fall in love with him, but I assure you it is really a waste of your time."

Neisa did not answer, but turned to look at her in surprise as it seemed such a curious remark to make.

"I have known Sheldon for a good long time," the Viscountess continued, "and he has told me that he does not intend to marry until he is quite old and then, of course, he must have a son. In the meantime, dear child, I want to save you a lot of heartache and unhappiness by telling you the truth."

Again Neisa made a little murmur. Words did not seem to come to her lips.

"So just take a look at some of the other charming young gentlemen, who are, I know, longing to marry you and I am sure you will be very happy – "

She rose as she spoke saying,

"And now I must go and tell the conquering hero how proud I am of him."

She did not wait for Neisa.

She climbed down from the stand and walked away towards the finishing post.

Neisa did not follow her.

She was still thanking God the Marquis was safe.

At the same time she felt as if there was a hollow emptiness in her breast that had not been there before.

CHAPTER FIVE

Luncheon had been arranged at the house for nearly fifty people.

When the large central table in the dining room was filled, there were smaller tables arranged to accommodate the overflow.

Neisa was hoping that she could avoid Randolph.

She had no sooner sat herself down at a small table, thinking that perhaps she should not push herself onto the large one, when he joined her.

There was only one other person at the table at that moment.

Randolph said in a low voice which only she could hear,

"I still want to know where you slept last night?"

She was so surprised at his asking her this question again that she looked at him in astonishment.

"I was with my cousin, as I told you before. We started to talk and we fell asleep."

She was not at all certain what the expression on Randolph's face meant.

Then she said, because she could not help it,

"Whatever I was doing, there is no reason for it to concern you."

"I wanted to talk to you last night and I want to talk to you today."

Neisa did not like the way he was speaking and she replied,

"I think it will be difficult until all the excitement is over."

He was about to respond when several other guests joined them at the table, so without any explanation Neisa rose and walked to the large table.

The Marquis was already seated at the head of the table and there was one seat left between two gentlemen with their backs to her and she quietly slipped into it.

They looked round, at first in surprise, and then in delight.

"We are very honoured you should join us," one of them piped up.

"I did not like the company at the table where I was sitting," muttered Neisa.

Even as she spoke she thought it was a somewhat indiscreet thing to have said and yet she felt she could not endure Randolph any longer.

She had a strong feeling that because his plan had not come off, he would make trouble one way or another and she did not want to be involved in it.

The gentlemen on either side set out to be amusing and interesting and she found the luncheon more enjoyable than she had expected.

She was aware that the Marquis was looking at her from time to time, but he was being totally monopolised by the Viscountess.

Neisa thought now she could understand why she had been warned against falling in love with him.

Of course, the Viscountess wanted him for *herself*!

So she had no wish for him to be spending his time with anyone else.

Neisa was not at all surprised to see that Carol and Sir Peter were alone at a small table, deep in conversation with each other.

Carol had seen Sir Peter pass the winning post with a number of the other horses.

She did not realise until the Marquis made a speech that after himself Sir Peter had been the winner.

"We must now all congratulate Sir Peter Jackson," he was saying. "He rode brilliantly and he must be all the more delighted that he was mounted on his own horse. He receives a special cup commemorating his victory and also the five hundred pounds which is the winner's prize."

Neisa knew that Sir Peter would be thrilled and the prize money would undoubtedly go towards financing his brilliant invention.

There were prizes for the second and third riders.

The third place had been a dead heat so the prize of one hundred pounds was divided between the two riders.

They all seemed very pleased with their prizes.

The Marquis spoke most generously in his speech of everyone who had taken part in his steeplechase.

He said he was thinking how he could make it even more difficult next year, if he was alive to do so.

As he uttered those last words, Neisa could not help looking at Randolph to see if he appeared uncomfortable or guilty in any way.

She had to turn round a little to look at him and to her surprise she could see that the seat where she had left him was now empty.

He had obviously gone away and she wondered if he had left Denholme Park altogether.

This seemed unlikely to her as he had been there when luncheon had started.

Then Neisa suddenly felt scared again.

Perhaps having failed to kill the Marquis at the fifth jump, he was setting a trap for him somewhere else.

Her partners at luncheon had told her that they all intended to ride over the jumps once again in the afternoon unless the Marquis had some different plan for them.

'Could it be possible,' Neisa asked herself, 'that Randolph has found out what they are intending to do and is determined to destroy the Marquis in some other way?'

She was so terrified that this might be his plan that she felt that she must warn the Marquis, however difficult it might be to do so.

After the Marquis's speech was finished, two other speeches were made to thank him most profusely for all his hospitality and most especially for the steeplechase.

It was then the Marquis announced,

"As the day is still young and you are all energetic, we should not waste our time talking about what we have just been doing, but what we should be doing next. I have therefore arranged that we shall have three races on my private Racecourse, starting in twenty minutes time."

There was a murmur of excitement round the table and then the riders began to clap their hands.

Everyone joined in the applause and the Marquis bowed and smiled before he sat down.

Neisa had not been aware, being so concerned with the steeplechase, that the Marquis had his own Racecourse.

Now she learned it was located on the other side of the stables beyond the paddocks and he had constructed it only last year.

As soon as luncheon was finished, the Marquis told all the riders to set off for the Racecourse and they could either ride their own horses or choose any of his to ride.

There was great excitement and as the riders surged to the door Neisa managed to reach the Marquis's side.

"*Please* be careful, my Lord," she pleaded, looking up at him and speaking so softly that he could hardly hear her.

"Of whom?" the Marquis enquired, she thought a little unnecessarily.

"He left the room in the middle of luncheon and I cannot think why, unless he was up to further mischief."

"Thank for the warning, Miss Waverton, but try not to worry."

"How can I help it?" implored Neisa.

He looked down at her and for a moment their eyes met.

Neisa felt that for some amazing reason she could not understand, her heart turned a somersault.

Then someone spoke to the Marquis and he moved away from her.

She next discovered that Carol had already set off in the direction of the Racecourse with Sir Peter and so she attached herself to Lady Sarah.

"I am not going to walk," insisted Lady Sarah, "so come with me in the pony cart, although I am sure at your age, it would be good for you to stretch your legs."

"I would much rather come with you, Lady Sarah."

They climbed into the pony cart that was driven by a young groom and they then set off for the Racecourse by a different route from those who were walking.

There were chairs near the winning post for those who wished to sit, but no stand as for the steeplechase.

Lady Sarah climbed out of the pony cart and made herself charming to the other ladies when they arrived.

Neisa sat in the back row of the chairs and watched the Marquis.

She became uncomfortably aware that there was no sign of Randolph.

In fact, he did not make an appearance until the first race was taking place.

He came from the direction of the house.

She thought, although she could not be sure, that, in that case, he had not been interfering with anything on the Racecourse.

He did not come near Neisa, sitting alone at the end of one of the rows of chairs and appeared to be scowling.

The races were fun and the Marquis by sheer hard riding was the victor in the first two races.

The third race was a handicap, so he and the other riders who had come in second and third places had to give a considerable start to those who had not been successful.

It was a very exciting race with everyone cheering when two young riders who had failed before came in first and second.

The Marquis produced a special prize for them.

What pleased them most was that they had defeated those who had won previously.

*

When it was time for tea, they returned to the house with Neisa travelling once again with Lady Sarah.

"It has been such an exciting day," enthused Neisa, as they drove off.

"I am very glad you have enjoyed it," Lady Sarah replied, "and may I tell you what a success you have been? Everyone has told me how charming they have found you and how very unspoilt you are."

Neisa smiled.

She could not help thinking that she had found very little in her life to spoil herself with before her arrival at Denholme Park.

Now disguised as her cousin, life was very different for her.

"I, also," Lady Sarah went on, "find Miss Moore delightful and I must remember to tell her just how much I enjoyed her father's last book. I thought it was brilliant."

Neisa was thinking it would please her father when she told him Lady Sarah had read and enjoyed *Journey's End*.

"He certainly has a good sense of humour," Lady Sarah continued. "I found myself laughing when the mule ran away with his baby daughter and he was frightened he would not catch up with it."

Neisa smiled.

How often she had heard that particular story which had happened to her when she was only one year old!

"I have recommended the book to very many of my friends," Lady Sarah was saying, "and I do hope that your uncle will be writing another one."

"I think he has nearly finished one."

"Oh, that is splendid! If you see him tell him how much I am looking forward to it."

"I will certainly do so, Lady Sarah."

They went into the house where there was a lavish tea waiting for them.

As some of the riders in the races had some way to go home, they started to say their goodbyes as soon as they had drunk a cup of tea.

"It has been such a glorious day," one after another

enthused to the Marquis as they shook his hand. "We will all be counting the days until next year."

"I will make it my business to ensure that you are not disappointed," replied the Marquis.

As he was speaking Neisa saw a little way behind him that Randolph was listening.

There was a grim expression on his face which she could only think of as evil and she felt a sharp stab of fear at what he might now be plotting.

One by one the guests who were not staying in the house took their leave.

At last there was only the house party left.

The ladies insisted that they now go upstairs to take off their hats and rest before dinner.

Because she thought she should go too, Neisa rose to her feet.

As she did so, the Marquis turned to her,

"I would like to speak to you, Miss Waverton – "

They walked together across the room and as they reached the fireplace where Randolph was standing alone, the Marquis addressed him curtly,

"Come to my study, Randolph. There is something I wish to say to you."

Randolph raised his bushy eyebrows at the Marquis as if he was surprised and replied mockingly,

"To hear is to obey, Master!"

Neisa wondered if the Marquis intended to take anyone else in with them, but apparently that was not in his mind.

They passed one or two of the house guests without a word.

When they reached his study they all three went in to the room and the Marquis closed the door behind them.

It was then that Neisa looked at the expression on his face and felt a little throb of anticipation that something unusual was about to happen.

Randolph was staring at the Marquis in a weird way and she thought he had a sinister look in his eyes.

And as she looked at him again she was almost sure he had taken drugs.

She had seen a number of drug addicts in the East with her father and although he had treated some of them, most were beyond his help – they were totally addicted to whatever drug they were taking.

She thought, although she could not see too clearly, that the pupils of his eyes were dark and enlarged and felt that she had been rather foolish not to suspect sooner that he was a drug taker.

He had given a poison pill to the Berber with which to kill the Marquis and he must, therefore, have access to a supply of drugs.

The Marquis walked to the mantelpiece and stood in front of it.

The fireplace was filled with flowers that looked very colourful against the white marble of the mantelpiece.

The whole room was one which Neisa particularly admired – there were huge bookcases against two of the walls and the pictures on the others were all of horses.

She recognised a magnificent Stubbs and thought it would be something her father would love to see. There was also his famous painting of cheetahs – animals she had seen in the East.

Because she thought it would be expected of her, she seated herself on the sofa on the right hand side of the fireplace.

She was expecting Randolph to sit down in one of the armchairs, but instead he stood behind one with his hands on the back of it as if he felt he needed support.

He was looking at the Marquis enquiringly.

For a moment no one spoke.

Then Randolph blurted out,

"This is rather like a Headmaster's study. Who is to get a caning this time?"

He spoke in a rude and jeering voice.

There was a short pause before the Marquis replied,

"I am afraid it is *you*, Randolph, and it is, I assure you, something that I find most unpleasant besides being incredible."

Randolph did not reply, but Neisa noticed that he stiffened.

"This morning," the Marquis went on quietly, "two Policemen arrested a man who was interfering with one of the jumps in the steeplechase.

"He was an Arab and he was found to be carrying drugs. He will be charged shortly with intending to maim or perhaps kill one of the horses and its rider, besides being in possession of illegal drugs."

Although the Marquis was speaking softly his voice seemed to fill the whole room.

Neither Randolph nor Neisa said a word.

"The Arab has informed the Policemen that he was acting on *your* instructions."

"It's all a monstrous lie!" Randolph shouted out at once. "A lie and I had nothing to do with it and I have no idea who this man is."

"As it so happens, he has been staying in this house and if necessary, the servants will identify him."

Randolph was, for the moment, taken aback.

Then he blurted out,

"If he is my servant, although I doubt it, I can only swear that I had nothing at all to do with his behaviour at the jumps and he has received no instructions from me."

"Unfortunately for you there is a witness who heard you actually giving the man the instruction he was carrying out. He was also told that when I fell, which I should have done, if the trap you set for me had worked, he was to give me a poison pill, which would have made sure I was dead in a few moments after it entered my mouth."

Randolph started.

Before he could speak, the Marquis looked at Neisa and asked,

"That is true, is it not, Miss Waverton."

"That is exactly – what I heard," Neisa answered in a low but calm voice.

"It is a lie! A damned lie!" yelled Randolph. "How on earth could this woman possibly have heard me? She is inventing the lie to cause trouble between us."

"Miss Waverton did hear you, Randolph, and she told me of your plans to make the fifth jump unjumpable. Now I am faced with a difficult decision as to what to do about you.

"I have only two alternatives. I can have you taken to the Police Station to confirm the story that your servant has already confessed to."

The Marquis paused before he continued,

"Alternatively, as I have no desire for any scandal in the family, I can make sure that you cannot do this sort of thing again."

He voice was sharp and he added scathingly,

"I have always known you were jealous of me and my title. I would never allow my family to be humiliated by having anyone who was a murderer at their head."

The Marquis's voice was now a whiplash.

Neisa thought that even Randolph, who was trying to look defiant, cringed for a moment.

Then Randolph snarled,

"If you denounce me, the family will suffer and the newspapers will make front page headlines of it."

"I am well aware of that possibility, Randolph, and I therefore offer you one chance of not going to prison."

"What is it?"

"That you go abroad immediately. In fact, that you leave this country within two hours and never come back. If you do, I will have you arrested for attempted murder."

Randolph gave out a loud gasp, but before he could speak, the Marquis carried on,

"Out of my kindness and because unfortunately we bear the same name, I will give you a thousand pounds a year payable through any bank you wish to name as long as you stay abroad. I am appalled by the way that you have behaved and I hope that I never see you again!"

The Marquis straightened his shoulders.

"Let me once again make this quite clear. If you ever do return, you will be arrested. Now go – a carriage is waiting for you outside with an escort to see you actually leave the country."

Almost as if he was hypnotised, Randolph moved from where he was standing.

The Marquis could not longer bear to look at him.

He turned round and placed his hands on the marble mantelpiece with his back towards Randolph as he walked slowly towards the door.

As he did so, Neisa rose from the sofa intending to stand beside the Marquis.

She wanted to comfort him in some way as she was aware how deeply shocked and upset he was that one of his own blood could have betrayed him and his family in such a disgusting way.

She sensed the hatred Randolph felt for him oozing out of his body almost as if she could see it.

It was then, as she stood up, that Randolph glanced at her.

She realised, as she saw the look in his eyes, that he was indeed heavily drugged.

He stood still.

Then, as if the idea came to him as a last resort, he drew a pistol from the inside pocket of his coat.

The Marquis with his back turned away had no idea of what was happening.

As Randolph began to raise his arm, Neisa knew at once what he was must do.

With a swiftness of a frightened animal, she gave a loud cry and flung herself against him.

He pulled the trigger but thanks to her brave action, the bullet hit the ceiling and not the Marquis.

He whipped round in total astonishment and saw at once what was happening.

Before Randolph could push Neisa away from him, the Marquis stuck him a hefty blow on the chin.

He fell backwards with a crash onto the ground.

As he did so, the study door was pulled open and the butler followed by two footmen rushed into the room.

"We heard a shot, my Lord," the butler exclaimed.

The Marquis pointed to Randolph on the floor with blood already pouring from his chin.

"Mr. Randolph here was showing us his pistol and it misfired. Carry him to the carriage outside. There is no time to lose."

Neisa realised that owing to the knockout blow and his head having crashed onto the floor as he fell, Randolph was unconscious.

The footmen picked him up and carried him out of the room.

The Marquis walked to his desk and put the pistol into one of the drawers.

"You have saved my life *again*, Miss Waverton," he sighed.

"How could you have known, how could you have possibly guessed that Randolph would be crazy enough to shoot you," she asked the Marquis in a frightened voice.

"I am unharmed and I can only say that I am more grateful than I can ever express to you, that you have taken me under your inspired protection."

There was a faint smile on his lips at the end of his speech.

Equally Neisa knew how upset he was and she felt the same.

She sat down heavily on the sofa and the Marquis said,

"I must see that Randolph is on his way. My night-watchmen, who are retired Policemen, are going with him. They will make sure that he leaves the country tonight."

He walked towards the door.

"Please stay here, Miss Waverton, and when I come back I will bring you something to drink."

He was gone before Neisa could blink an eyelid.

She thought it was only by a miracle that she had been able to save him.

How could anyone have guessed or even imagined that Randolph would be crazy enough to shoot the Marquis down in cold blood?

It would be impossible for him to extricate himself from such a crime.

'Thank you God, thank you so very much God,' she murmured as the door closed.

The Marquis had not returned within the next ten minutes and Neisa thought it would be tactful if she went upstairs and lay down.

She could see quite a number of potent difficulties that would need to be quickly overcome where Randolph was concerned.

If any of the house party became aware of the scene they would talk.

There would have to be many explanations and lies to explain as to what had actually been the serious crime of attempted murder.

She walked up the back staircase and reaching her bedroom, she undressed herself without ringing for Hannah and lay down on her bed.

She had not been there for long before Carol came bustling in.

"I wondered where you were, Neisa, it is sensible of you to lie down before dinner."

"Did you enjoy the steeplechase?" Neisa enquired. "You must have been pleased that Sir Peter won."

"He is delighted with himself and he thinks that it is a special omen that his invention will now be accepted by the Admiralty."

"I feel sure it will be."

"You look very tired," Carol commented. "I had better leave you and maybe you will be able to sleep before dinner. There is plenty of time."

"I would like a little nap," Neisa agreed.

She was worried that Carol might ask her questions about what had happened this evening.

Apparently she was totally unaware that Randolph had been taken from the house and Neisa could only hope that the same could be said for the other guests.

She was still feeling apprehensive.

Unlikely though it was, Randolph might somehow manage to sneak back into the house and try once again to kill the Marquis.

'He was drugged to his eyeballs and when people are drugged they will do anything, however stupid,' Neisa told herself.

This was no excuse nor did it make it any safer for the Marquis to move about on his estate.

She lay in bed staring at the ceiling thinking about him.

She must have been in her room for nearly half-an-hour when there was a knock on the communicating door between her room and the boudoir.

She knew without being told who it was.

As she called out,

"Come in," she sat up in bed.

It was the Marquis.

As he walked towards her, she saw the expression on his face was no longer grim and angry, as it had been when he was rampaging at Randolph.

"What has happened now, my Lord?" she asked as the Marquis reached her.

"I knew you would be worrying, that is why I came to tell you that everything is now all right and I want you to try to forget what has occurred today."

"It will be quite impossible to do so, but how could we have guessed that he kept a loaded pistol in his pocket and was determined to kill you one way or another?"

"I find it hard to believe myself," said the Marquis, "but I cannot allow you to be upset."

He sat down on the side of her bed.

He was thinking as he did so that no one could look lovelier or more concerned for him.

"You have been so wonderful," he breathed. "Now you have to remember it is all over and never think about it again."

"How *can* it be all over?"

"What I have told you is not the whole story. His Berber servant was not arrested by the Police, but by two of my staff who were in the Police Force until they came to me. One of them had at one time worked in the East and has a smattering of Arabic."

He paused for a moment.

"He received confirmation with some difficulty of what you had told me had been Randolph's instructions. The Berber also had a considerable quantity of drugs on his person, some of which I imagine he takes himself."

"And so does your cousin Randolph."

"I thought you would realise that. I have suspected for a long time it was something he indulged in."

"But you know how dangerous those drugs are."

"Yes, I do, but I am somewhat surprised that you should know."

With a little start Neisa now remembered that she was pretending to be Carol.

Her cousin had not been to the East as she had. Nor had her father treated men who had been drug addicts for many years.

Because she feared she might give herself away she said quickly,

"What have you done with Randolph?"

"When I realised how deeply unconscious he was, I think more from the drugs he was taking than from my fist, I knew we should be rid of him immediately."

Neisa was listening with her eyes on the Marquis.

"I sent the two men who had been in charge of his servant and him to London straight away. They are now travelling with four horses and should be there in plenty of time to catch the first ship leaving Tilbury for Rotterdam.

"If Randolph wishes to live in France when he has recovers, that is his own business. I gave my men enough money to give him so he can make his arrangements and be comfortable for at least a month."

"And after that, he will receive the allowance you promised him?"

"Of course, and I do believe that he will be sensible enough to obey my commands to stay abroad. If he comes back here, it will be impossible for me not to worry as to when he will turn up and kill me when I least expect it."

Neisa gave a little cry.

"It must not happen! Oh, please do make sure that he obeys you. He is so weird and I don't trust him."

"Nor do I, but all thanks to you, Miss Waverton, he has learned his lesson and it will be some time before he approaches me again."

Neisa thought that this sounded unconvincing.

Whatever the Marquis might maintain there would always be the fear that he was lurking in the garden behind a tree!

He would never give up his evil schemes to kill the Marquis so that he could take his position and title.

She knew only too well, both from what her father had told her and what she had seen herself that people who took drugs were completely reckless. They were incapable of thinking out the likely results of their actions before they did anything.

"You are not to look worried," urged the Marquis. "I promise you that I will take every precaution, and, if it is necessary I will arrange for Randolph to be watched so that if he suddenly dreams up a new way of assassinating me, I shall be forewarned."

"Oh, do so, my Lord! Please promise you will do! I *cannot* feel happy unless you are safe."

"Does it really matter to you whether I am or not?"

The Marquis spoke very gently and Neisa felt that she had spoken too ardently and blushed.

He rose from the bed.

"I must allow you to rest, but I want you to enjoy yourself tonight and look very beautiful for my party. We are going to dance to an unusual and brilliant band. And because we have a secret between us, which no one else knows, I claim the first dance."

Neisa gave a chuckle.

"I will promise you that and you do swear that what you have told me is true? There is no chance of Randolph blowing up the house or making the roof of the ballroom fall in on us?"

She was speaking lightly, but there was still a note in her voice that told the Marquis she was still perturbed.

"Leave everything to me. Tomorrow we can enjoy a quiet day and talk on subjects we both enjoy."

"Which is, of course, Champion, my Lord!"

"He excelled himself today. In fact, I have never known him jump so well or run so swiftly."

He moved towards the door and then he stopped.

"I suppose, Miss Waverton, that the best way I can show my gratitude, which I can assure you is very sincere, is to let you ride Champion!"

Neisa clasped her hands together.

"Do you mean it?"

"Yes, I really mean it, and it would be, I feel, of considerable more value to you than if I was to buy you a diamond necklace."

"*Much* more valuable!" agreed Neisa.

She realised that the Marquis was thinking that she could easily buy herself a diamond necklace with all the money she was supposed to have.

But only *he* could lend her Champion.

He left the room and Neisa lay back on the pillows with a sigh of satisfaction.

'He is so very kind,' she reflected, 'and it would be ghastly if that horrible Randolph had succeeded in taking his place and become the owner of this beautiful house!'

And he would also be the owner of Champion and all the other horses.

The mere idea made her shudder.

She closed her eyes.

As she did so, she was wondering if the Marquis remembered that the first time he had said he was grateful to her he had kissed her.

She knew, although she scarcely liked to admit it, that she desperately wanted him to kiss her again.

CHAPTER SIX

Neisa was just beginning to dress herself for dinner when Carol came hurrying into her room.

She looked at her in surprise, as she was expecting Hannah after she had dressed Carol first.

Carol, however, was in a new and pretty day frock, but not an evening gown.

Before she could comment, Carol blurted out,

"Listen Neisa! I am not coming to dinner tonight. I am going out with Peter."

"Going out?" Neisa exclaimed in astonishment.

"He wants to show me his house. It is only two or three miles from here and which is why he and the Marquis have been friends ever since they were small boys."

"You are going to see his house and dine there with him," asked Neisa, as if she was trying to get it clear in her own mind.

"I have written a note to the Marquis apologising. I want to be with Peter and he is very keen for me to see his home."

"I am sure he is," smiled Neisa.

Carol gave her a kiss and without saying any more hurried away.

When she had departed, Neisa thought it was rather odd for her to go out to dinner while she was staying with the Marquis as his guest.

She suspected, however, that he would understand.

At the same time she felt it would make Carol more in love with Sir Peter Jackson than she was already and that definitely worried her.

It was a considerable cause for concern, but there was nothing she could do about it.

Hannah came along a little later and helped her put on a very pretty gown she had not worn before.

"Miss Carol suggested that in case any of tonight's guests have met her before, it'd be wise if you disguised yourself a little."

"What does she mean?" asked Neisa astonished.

"We were thinking how it could be done, miss, and I remembered that one of the dresses had a wreath with it. Now you and Miss Carol look a little alike, but a wreath'll make a huge difference with your hair arranged in the same way."

"I see, Hannah, and it would be a terrible disaster if someone arrived and said that I was not Carol."

She recognised that it undoubtedly would annoy the Marquis and she had no wish to upset him at the moment when he had Randolph to worry about and the necessity of keeping his disgraceful plot a secret.

Hannah therefore arranged a very pretty wreath of roses on Neisa's head.

It actually did make her look quite different from how she had looked for the last two days.

However, when she walked downstairs Neisa found she had worried unnecessarily.

When the Marquis introduced her to the newcomers she learned they were all near neighbours and were fully engaged with horses and the countryside.

They were definitely not the smart fortune-seekers she had heard so much about in London.

It did not seem to perturb the Marquis that two of his guests would be missing dinner.

There were, in fact, a large number of new guests and more arrived after they had gone into the ballroom.

This was a room which Neisa had not seen before and she was impressed with its white columns and cornices picked out in gold leaf.

She only wished she could tell someone that this was her first ball and she was feeling as excited as a child at her first pantomime.

The Marquis claimed the first dance as he had told her he intended to do.

The Viscountess was obviously extremely put out.

"I thought you always danced the first dance with me, Sheldon," she hissed reproachfully as the Marquis put his arm round Neisa's waist.

"That was when we were in London, Sheila, and in other people's houses. Tonight I am dancing with my most important guest because, as I have already indicated, her father was most generous to me when I was visiting New York."

It was a very reasonable explanation, but Neisa was aware that the Viscountess was looking at her crossly.

She tossed her head as she stalked away.

The Marquis now swept Neisa round the room and she could understand, as he was such a good dancer, that every lady would wish to dance with him.

She was a little afraid, as she had only danced with her father or with elderly foreigners that she would make a fool of herself.

"You are as light as thistledown," he murmured and she knew it was a genuine compliment.

She longed to tell him it was the first time she had ever danced in an English ballroom with an Englishman.

But that was something she must not do and so she concentrated on enjoying the dance.

"What are you thinking about?" the Marquis asked her unexpectedly.

"I was just thinking, my Lord, how lucky I am to be dancing with you."

She spoke without thinking and then as she felt that her comment might sound too personal, she added quickly,

"You are a very good dancer."

"And you are a very good judge, Miss Waverton."

"I hope – so," mumbled Neisa.

This enchanting dance in this stately ballroom was something that she would always remember when she had returned to the Vicarage and there were no more balls.

They waltzed for what seemed a long time and then the Marquis whispered into her ear,

"Now I must go and be a good host, but you must keep me several dances before the night ends."

Neisa smiled at him.

As they came to a standstill, three young gentlemen rushed up to claim the next dance.

Although she did not wish to feel cynical, she could not help wondering whether they would have all asked her with such enthusiasm if they had not known she was rich.

She sensed that the Vicar's daughter would not be in such demand, but she longed to dance again and again.

She had so many aspiring partners that they decided they would adopt the American habit of 'cutting-in.'

This meant they could all have a turn with her.

It was all very thrilling and Neisa had no idea that her eyes were shining brightly.

As she went from partner to partner, her excitement and enjoyment was infectious.

"It is such a pleasure," Lady Sarah murmured to the Marquis, "to see anyone enjoy herself as much as the little heiress. One might think after being feted in London she might be somewhat blasé. Instead her enjoyment seems to vibrate through the room and has become infectious."

The Marquis laughed.

"You are right, Aunt Sarah, and it is surprising how unspoilt she is, considering the fuss that has been made of her."

He was thinking to himself that in her delight at the ball, she would soon forget the drama that had taken place earlier in his study.

He still found it very hard to believe.

Yet if she had not been so exceptionally brave and intervened when Randolph aimed his pistol at his back, he would now be a dead man.

'That is twice now she has saved me,' the Marquis told himself, 'and I pray to God there will not be any need for her to do so again.'

He still could not help hoping that there had been no difficulties in the carriage going to London.

It was true that the two men escorting Randolph were Police Officers, who had each been in the local force for over ten years.

The Marquis had persuaded them to take over the security of the house, especially at night, as it held so many fabulous treasures that were constantly being written about in the newspapers.

He was very conscious of how incredibly valuable his treasures were.

The two Police Officers were only too delighted, as their homes were in the village, to resign from the force.

The job the Marquis offered them was much better paid and they had proved excellent men in every way.

He recognised they would be shocked and horrified at Randolph's extraordinary behaviour.

Not only in instructing his manservant, the Berber, to try to kill him and Champion during the steeplechase, but also in attempting to shoot him when he had instructed him to leave England.

The only excuse for his behaviour was that he was under the influence of drugs and he rebuked himself for not having realised it sooner. As he looked back he felt that he should have known a long time ago that Randolph was an addict.

There were so many indications which should have prompted him to find it out earlier.

'Heaven knows what will happen to him when he lives abroad,' the Marquis wondered.

Then he decided that he should not worry himself about Randolph anymore and enjoy his party.

They danced until one o'clock to the excellent band that everyone said was the best they had ever heard.

Then the Marquis pronounced that it was now time for everyone to retire to bed – and he was thinking more of Neisa than of anyone else.

She looked very happy and appeared to be enjoying herself enormously.

Yet he knew that anyone who was at all sensitive was bound to be adversely affected by the terrible events she had been involved in during the last twenty-four hours.

He realised too, and it was very touching, that she was concerned about him.

The band next played 'God Save the Queen', and everyone stood to attention.

Then they all seemed to be talking at once as they thanked the Marquis for the ball and the steeplechase.

"It has been a wonderful day, my Lord," the guests enthused one after another.

The ladies looked up at him with a softness in their eyes which told him how much they admired him.

Only when the last guest had left did the Marquis give a sigh of relief.

"Now everyone, don't waste time. We all need our beauty sleep. Come on Aunt Sarah, you should have been in bed ages ago!"

"I enjoyed every moment tonight even though I am too old to dance," Lady Sarah replied. "But I shall hope to enjoy a very good night's sleep before Church tomorrow. If anyone wants to come with me, I will be leaving at a quarter to eleven."

Neisa realised that the Viscountess and other ladies in the party did not reply to her – and instead they moved rather quickly towards the stairs.

She moved to Lady Sarah's side.

"I would love to come with you, Lady Sarah, if I may."

"Of course you can, child, and I shall be delighted to take you."

She gave a little smile as she added,

"I think we will be on our own with the exception of Sheldon who always reads the lesson."

Neisa smiled.

It was what she would have expected him to do and she knew that her father would approve.

She did not say any more, but walked upstairs with Lady Sarah, while the Marquis was saying goodnight to the band.

She thought, as she undressed, that she would have liked to have said goodnight to him.

It had been very different last night when she had been frightened of Randolph coming to her bedroom and the Marquis had been so kind and so understanding about where she slept.

Then he had come to tell her what had happened to Randolph.

She would not feel embarrassed if he came again, but there was no sign of him.

After she said her prayers, she blew out the candles and fell asleep.

*

When she woke in the morning, she was expecting Hannah to enter her and call her.

To her surprise Carol came in. She walked across the room and pulled back the curtains.

Neisa sat up in bed.

"Good morning, Carol. I was not expecting you so early," she mumbled.

"I have something to tell you, Neisa."

She walked back from the window and then sat on the side of the bed.

"We are leaving this afternoon after luncheon."

Neisa's eyes widened.

"After luncheon?" she repeated. "But I thought we were staying until Monday."

Carol was silent for a moment, and as Neisa looked into her face, she asked breathlessly,

"What has happened?"

"As I told you, I went to see Peter's house last night and it was just as fascinating as I thought it would be."

"Is it as big as this?"

"No. It is much smaller because it is Elizabethan and very lovely."

She gave a deep sigh.

"It's a house I could be very happy in."

"And what happened?" Neisa asked again.

"I realised that Peter had taken me to see his home because he wanted me to love it. And I *did* love it, Neisa. It is perfect, the sort of house I would want for myself and where I could make a wonderful home for my husband and my children."

There was a pain in Carol's voice and Neisa knew there was nothing she could say.

"We looked round all the rooms first and then we had supper in his pretty dining room. I have no idea what I ate as I was so happy being with Peter. Everything seemed like the ambrosia of the Gods!"

"Then what – ?" Neisa persisted, knowing it must have been something disastrous.

"A messenger arrived unexpectedly from London. He was from the First Lord of the Admiralty."

Again there was a long pause until Carol went on,

"The First Lord asked him to come to London early this morning, because he has to go abroad on Monday."

"I hope that means that they are going to accept Sir Peter's invention?"

"That is what Peter thought and, of course, he was terribly excited."

She put her hands up to her eyes as she spoke as if she was remembering every word he had said.

Then as she could not help herself, the words came tumbling from her lips.

"He kissed me and told me he loved me. He also

said that today when he gets back from London – although it might be late – he has something most important to ask me."

Carol's voice seemed to die away.

Neisa muttered almost in a whisper,

"He is going to ask you to marry him."

There was another long pause until Carol sobbed,

"He is going – to ask *you* – Neisa. The little girl from the Vicarage, the Vicar's daughter – to be his wife."

There was an unmistakable agony in Carol's voice and Neisa suggested quickly,

"I am certain that he will understand when you tell him who you are."

Carol shook her head.

"He said over and over again he would never marry anyone who had more money than he has and he intends to stand on his own feet and make his invention work."

"But Carol, darling – " Neisa began.

Carol put up her hands.

"There is nothing to say, so do not argue with me. I know exactly how Peter is feeling and I just cannot face the moment when he turns away from me, and tells me he has no wish to ever see me again."

"But he cannot do that!" protested Neisa.

"He will and I am *not* strong enough to bear it."

"So what are you going to do?"

"I am going back to America. I could not stay in England and be near Peter without seeing him. It would be agony – a worse agony than I am feeling now. Perhaps it will not be so bad when the Atlantic is between us."

The distraught tone in Carol's voice hurt Neisa.

"We are therefore leaving, Neisa, immediately after luncheon. I shall tell the Marquis that my father has sent for me because something has happened in the village.

"He will not know or care whether there has been a message for me or that I have sent for our carriage. You must say that you will come with me, Neisa."

"Of course I will, but, dearest Carol, are you really doing the right thing? Would it perhaps be better to wait and see?"

"I think if I saw the dislike in Peter's eyes when he knows that I have deceived him and heard him say that he no longer loved me, I would want to die!"

Her voice broke, but she continued,

"I have to be brave, because I knew I was falling in love with Peter and this was bound to happen."

Neisa gave a little cry.

"*Why*? Oh, why, did we pretend to be each other?"

"It is something I have enjoyed more than I have ever enjoyed anything else in my whole life. It has been wonderful to feel that I had found a man who loves me for myself and not for that pile of money sitting in the bank."

She rose from the bed and walked to the window and stood looking out.

The morning sun was shining through her hair and Neisa thought it made her look tragically unworldly.

"Now I realise what love is," Carol sighed, as if she was speaking to herself. "If I never find it again, at least I shall have something to remember for the rest of my life."

Because the scene was so heartbreaking, Neisa felt tears come into her eyes.

"Oh, Carol dearest, what can I say, what can I do?"

"*Nothing*. Except help me to leave without there being too much fuss about it."

She walked towards the door.

"I have told Hannah to pack my bags and when she has finished mine, she will do yours."

She did not wait for Neisa to reply, but closed the door behind her.

Neisa put her hands up to her eyes.

She loved Carol and could not bear her to suffer so acutely. Yet what could she do about it?

If Sir Peter was so absolutely determined never to be dependent upon any woman who had so much money, how could they ever be happy?

There was no obvious answer to that question.

When Hannah came to her room later, Neisa knew by the expression on her face how upset she was because Carol was so unhappy.

It was a relief, as they had been so late last night, that there were only a few gentlemen at breakfast.

They were all talking about riding and one or two were determined to go over the steeplechase course again.

"I cannot imagine how our host will improve on it by next year," one of them was saying, "but he is so clever he will undoubtedly succeed in doing so."

"I am going to race if anyone will challenge me on the Racecourse," another suggested.

Neisa was longing to join in, but she reckoned that her father would be shocked if she did not go to Church on Sunday.

She could only wonder if it would be at all possible for her to be given a ride before she was obliged to leave.

At a quarter to eleven the Marquis's best carriage was outside the front door waiting for Lady Sarah.

When Neisa joined her, she was rather surprised to see there was no sign of the Marquis.

"Sheldon has gone on ahead," Lady Sarah told her, as if she had asked the question. "He always likes to have a good look at the lesson before he has to read it."

"Is your Church a very old one?" asked Neisa.

"It was built at the very same time as the house was remodelled by the Adam brothers and there is a Chapel, which I do not think you have seen, in the house itself."

"No one has told me about it."

"That is because it is currently being renovated and will, I think, be as beautiful is it was originally by the time Sheldon has finished with it."

"I would really love to see the Chapel."

"I am sure you can and I may tell you that Sheldon is very proud of the alterations he has made. I think it is unusual in a young man for him to take so much interest."

Neisa thought the same.

When they entered the Church she saw the Marquis standing at the lectern turning over the pages of the large Bible.

Neisa felt a sudden and unusual excitement rising within her that she could not control.

The Marquis looked so handsome and she realised that reading the lesson was important to him – it was what few young gentlemen of such distinction would feel.

'He is a very remarkable man,' she told herself.

She and Lady Sarah entered the family pew.

As they knelt to pray, Neisa admitted to herself that she loved the Marquis.

She had given him both her heart and soul.

She had not intended to.

She had known only too well, as the Viscountess had told her, that it was just hopeless for her to fall in love with anyone from a different world to her own.

She could well understand that the Marquis would not want to be married until he was a great deal older.

He wanted to enjoy himself as most men would.

Beautiful ladies like the Viscountess all fawned on him and, Neisa pondered, were only too willing to fall into his arms.

She felt, as she ruminated about it, as if she had stabbed herself and the knife had made a hole in her heart.

'*I love him*, I love him,' her mind told her.

Just to look at him made a thrill course through her whole body.

Yet she knew quite well it was hopeless – she was reaching for the moon, the sun and the stars.

At the same time she could no longer prevent her love from running through her veins than she could from breathing.

The service started and the choir sang like angels.

Looking round, Neisa knew the Marquis had spent money on his local Church.

She was quite certain that the Vicar, who looked well fed, enjoyed a large stipend.

There were quite a number of people in the Church.

The Marquis read the second lesson in a deep and sincere voice which seemed to demand attention.

Even the children did not fidget but listened.

Neisa could only look at him to know her love was hopeless, but in any event it was the most beautiful feeling she had ever experienced in her life.

It was everything that she felt in the woods, found in the flowers and heard in the song of the birds.

It was the starlight at night, the moon creeping into her bedroom.

It was the sun in the morning, bringing a feeling of youth and vitality.

It was a love which embraced the whole world and what she could never feel again for another man.

When the service was over the Marquis sent away his own chaise which had brought him to the Church.

He then joined his Aunt and Neisa to drive back to the house with them.

"I am afraid," he smiled, "that you and I have had to pray for the whole party. When I suggested they should join us, they each had some other well thought out excuse for not doing so!"

Lady Sarah laughed.

"You expect far too much, Sheldon! I feel sure that Miss Waverton's prayers have made up for all those who were missing."

"That is something I thought myself."

He smiled at Neisa as he spoke.

She felt as if her heart was spinning round in her breast. And the sun was more brilliant than it had been a moment earlier.

*

When they reached the house, Lady Sarah went to her room and the Marquis turned to Neisa,

"I am sorry to learn that there is trouble for your cousin at home and that you have to leave us earlier than you intended."

"I-I am sorry too, my Lord."

"I hope we will meet in London. I expect you will be returning there and I intend to pay a visit to my London house sometime this week."

Neisa did not answer and after a moment or two, he suggested,

"Perhaps we can take luncheon or dinner together either in your house or mine. I have so much to say to you that is impossible to do here with so many people around."

"That – would be very delightful," Neisa managed to reply, although she knew it would never happen.

She went up to her room to find everything packed, expect the dress she was travelling in.

"All this rush, rush, rush!" Hannah grumbled away crossly. "It'll do no one no good. Where's all the hurry, I keeps asking myself?"

Neisa had no wish to leave.

She longed to stay with the Marquis for as long as she could.

She recognised deep in her heart that once they had departed from Denholme Park after luncheon, she would never see him again.

Carol had said she would be leaving immediately for America. Therefore when the Marquis called at the big house in Park Lane, he would be told she had gone.

She did not believe that he would give her another thought.

She walked slowly and forlornly downstairs just as the Marquis was coming in through the front door.

He called out to Neisa,

"You must have forgotten that I had promised you a ride on Champion. It is nearly time for luncheon and I feel that if you are going to leave shortly afterwards, it will be impossible for you to ride and drive at the same time."

He was smiling, but Neisa wanted to cry out that she was losing something wonderful!

It was agonising to say that he was right.

"I have, however, thought of a compromise, Miss Waverton. Perhaps you would be my guest again, if not next weekend, then the weekend after. We could make it just a quiet party and perhaps your father will have retuned to England by then – "

Neisa could not answer him and after a moment he continued,

"I am sure that Champion will be looking forward to you riding him as eagerly as you are and I always keep my promises. So you *must* keep yours!"

It was what Neisa wanted to do more than she ever wanted anything in her whole life.

Yet she kept telling herself that he was only being polite.

When he learned she was not Mr. Waverton's little daughter, he would then soon wipe her out of his mind and never think of her again.

She managed, however, to respond with difficulty,

"It is most kind of you – and of course – I will be counting – the days and hours until I can see Champion again."

"Since he cannot do that for himself, I will do it for him," the Marquis twinkled.

She gave him a weak smile, but because it was such agony to do so, it was not very successful.

They then had reached the door of the room where everyone was congregating before luncheon.

As they went in, Neisa was aware they were all still talking about horses.

At luncheon she sat on the left side of the Marquis, who was again being monopolised by the Viscountess.

Neisa had to endure a gentleman on her other side who was determined to call on her at what he thought was her father's house in Park Lane.

He was very keen to meet Mr. Waverton, as he was planning to visit New York imminently and thought that an acquaintance with such an influential businessman would be greatly to his advantage.

He made it very clear to Neisa that he intended to invite her to a luncheon or dinner party as soon as it could be arranged.

She had the greatest difficulty in avoiding giving him the date he required.

She found herself listening to the caressing voice of the Viscountess telling the Marquis how wonderful he was.

With sophisticated and captivating women like her, Neisa thought, he would never have taken any notice of her if she had not saved his life.

She started when the Marquis turned to her,

"And what are you thinking about Miss Waverton? You are very quiet."

"I was thinking that so much happened yesterday that if we wrote it in a book, no one would believe us!"

"That's very right," agreed the Marquis, "but it is a book I would have no wish to read!"

"Nor would I," added Neisa.

Once again the Viscountess attracted his attention and once again Neisa found herself wondering if Randolph had reached the Continent.

Or if the two men in charge of him had experienced any difficulties. She knew that when she left, it would be unlikely she would ever hear of Randolph again.

Although she was glad, it meant that she would not see the Marquis again either.

She glanced at him and could see the Viscountess whispering something in his ear.

Her hand, with its long white fingers, was resting on his as she did so.

'I suppose,' thought Neisa, 'that is flirting, which is something I have never learned to do.'

She decided that what she felt for the Marquis was not just something intriguing or something to laugh about.

It was something serious and holy.

It was a love that she believed came from God.

Then she told herself she was being ridiculous.

Men like the Marquis were always being pursued by pretty women, amused by them and perhaps infatuated with them.

They did not want to be serious.

They wanted to enjoy life and to remain free.

Only the requirement for an heir would force them into marriage.

There was no need for him to marry anyone rich. Nor for that matter someone who had a talent which he did not have himself.

He had *everything*!

What had anyone like herself to offer him?

'I am certainly presuming too much and asking too much,' Neisa determined.

"You must let me meet your father," the man on the left was saying. "And of course I want to see you again. You are so very beautiful, and I wanted, before you left, to have a chance to talk to you seriously."

"What about?" Neisa asked without thinking.

"About you and me," the man replied. "But this is not the right place, it is just not romantic enough for what I have to say."

For a moment Neisa could not think what he was

talking about and then she realised he was on the verge of proposing to her.

It was something she did not wish to happen and under the circumstances, it would be very embarrassing.

She turned to the Marquis.

"As I have to leave so soon, would it be possible for me to say goodbye to Champion?" she enquired.

He smiled at her.

"Of course you can, but it has to be only *au revoir*. Promise me that you will come down the weekend I have suggested. You can then ride him on the Racecourse and I might even race you."

"I think Champion would be very upset if you won. In fact, he would think he had been defrauded!"

"We might risk it, but if you want to see him, come along now before your carriage for London arrives."

Neisa did not tell him that Carol would be dropping her off first at Little Meadowfield.

She was secretly hoping, as Carol was so obviously unhappy, to persuade her to stay the night.

However, she had a strong feeling that Carol would want to put as many miles between herself and Sir Peter as possible.

Neisa could well understand that she was terrified of having to listen to a hard note in his voice and seeing a very different expression in his eyes.

It was *money*! There was a mountain of money standing between them.

It separated them more completely than any frontier wall.

Then the Marquis rose, made excuses to his aunt and told everyone not to hurry from the table.

He escorted Neisa to the stables.

There was no one about as it was luncheon time not only for the gentry but also for the grooms.

The Marquis opened the door of Champion's stall and they went in.

The great horse heard his voice and moved towards him. He nuzzled against him in a very touching way.

"He loves you," exclaimed Neisa.

"I often think more than anyone else has ever loved me," responded the Marquis.

Neisa looked at him in surprise.

"Why do you say that?"

"Because Champion loves me just for myself – not for my title, my possessions or anything I can give him. I honestly don't think he associates me with the food he eats or the water he drinks."

"Of course not," agreed Neisa.

"How often can you say the same about people?" the Marquis asked. "No one knows better than you do the penalty of having so much that one is never sure how much it counts when weighed against the feelings of the heart."

"I do know – exactly what – you are now saying."

She was thinking of all the money that was making Carol's life so miserably unhappy – so much money that was causing her to run away so that she would not have to face the look in Sir Peter's eyes.

It suddenly stuck Neisa that she was so incredibly lucky in a way she had never counted before.

No one could ever love her except for herself since she possessed nothing.

She really longed to tell the Marquis the truth, but it might make it matters worse for Carol.

Even if she then swore him to secrecy, it would be embarrassing to admit that they had both deceived him.

They had not been honest enough as he might have expected them to be.

'I love him beyond peradventure,' she murmured to herself. 'I love him as I shall never love anyone else and this is the *last* time I shall see him.'

She bent forward to pat Champion again.

He pushed his nose against her hand in a friendly gesture.

She had the feeling, strange though it might seem, that he understood her predicament.

More completely and more kindly than the Marquis would ever be able to do!

CHAPTER SEVEN

The Marquis said goodbye to Carol and Neisa.

"It has been a real joy having you here," he said to Neisa. "As I told you, I am coming to London this week, perhaps Wednesday or Thursday and I will call and hope to see you."

Neisa smiled wistfully at him.

When he said goodbye to Carol, she forced herself to thank him for the delightful visit.

And only Neisa was aware that she was very near to tears and her voice sounded hoarse.

They drove away down the drive.

It was with difficulty that Neisa did not glance back to see if the Marquis was watching them leave.

Carol was saying a desperate goodbye to everything that really mattered to her and she was doing the same.

She wondered if they would have been happier if they had not come to Denholme Park in the first place.

She knew what she felt about the Marquis and what Carol was feeling about Sir Peter was something neither of them would ever forget.

This weekend would influence them for the rest of their lives.

'There could never be another man as wonderful as the Marquis,' Neisa told herself over and over again.

Then she too felt like weeping, but tears were not going to help.

There was life to be lived without the two men they loved – they had appeared in their lives so unexpectedly and just as unexpectedly were fading away.

They drove in silence for quite a long distance.

Then Carol sobbed,

"I feel as if nothing will ever matter again – and the world is completely and absolutely empty."

"Things will get better" Neisa tried to comfort her. "You will find new interests and new people in America to meet and forget entirely that England has only brought you unhappiness."

"Papa will be disappointed. In fact I think he will be very angry with me."

"I know he only wants you to have the best – as he loves you so much. If you explain to him why you have returned so quickly to America, he will understand."

"I just cannot tell him that Peter will not marry me because I have too much money," moaned Carol. "Papa would take it as an insult. He has worked so hard because he loved my mother. He wanted to be successful only so that he could lay his triumphs at her feet."

Neisa thought that was undoubtedly true.

She recalled that when her father had experienced anything exceptional, like healing a man who had been left to die, the first person he wanted to tell how successful he had been was her mother.

It was certainly something that would never be said by the Marquis.

He had everything and he did not have to strive to make himself any richer or more significant.

Then she recalled the Viscountess's words.

He would eventually require an heir to carry on the ancient title and the legacy of the Denholme lineage and he would also need as his wife someone whose blood was as blue as his.

His marriage would be a great occasion whenever or wherever it took place.

Because it hurt Neisa so to think about the Marquis, she forced herself to ignore her own troubles and focus on Carol's.

"What you must do, darling, is to try to spend your money in a way where it will do good to other people."

"My Papa has already thought of that. He has built schools in all sorts of unlikely places, and just before I left, he was contemplating financing a University."

"Quite right! That is exactly what he should do!" cried Neisa.

"So you see," Carol replied in a gloomy voice, "no one really wants me."

Neisa wanted to say she was sure Sir Peter would miss her.

Then she thought such a remark might make things worse. They therefore drove on in silence until they came to the village of Little Meadowfield.

"Do stay the night with me, Carol," Neisa pleaded, as the gates of the Vicarage came into sight.

"I will if you want me – miserable though I am. I don't think at the moment I could face the prospect of Lady Margrave chattering on about how many new suitors she has found for me."

Carol's voice was scathing.

"No, of course not. Just stay quietly here. You will find Papa will be so immersed in his book, he will not even realise we have been away."

The horses came to a standstill outside the Vicarage front door.

Carol climbed out first and said to the coachmen,

"It is too late now to carry on to London. Will you find somewhere local to stay? I expect I will go up either tomorrow morning or immediately after luncheon."

"Very good, miss," the coachman touched his hat.

Carol walked into the house and Neisa looked back to see if there was any sign of the groom who was bringing Hannah and the luggage.

She had hoped that Carol might stay the night at the Vicarage and had therefore warned Hannah that she might not be as comfortable as she had been at Denholme Park.

"Don't you worry about me, miss," Hannah replied. "I've roughed it in me life and it's only thankful I am for a soft bed to lie down on, now I'm getting old."

Neisa had laughed.

"You deserve every comfort, Hannah, and that is what I wish I could give you."

"It's Miss Carol you has to worry about."

The Waverton carriage turned round and drove off.

She and Carol walked into the sitting room and sat down.

"I am going to be a dispirited visitor, Neisa, and if you were wise, you would have sent me on to London."

"I am being wise in keeping you with me, and you are to stay with me for just as long as you like."

She left Carol to find her father and found him, as she had anticipated, in the study working on his book.

"Hello, my dear!" he exclaimed as she came into the room. "I was not expecting you back until tomorrow."

"I know, Papa, but Carol has a party in London and wishes to stay with us tonight so as not to make the journey too tiring."

She realised as she made the explanation that her father was not listening.

"I have just finished my book," he trumpeted.

"You have, Papa? How splendid!"

"I only have to make a few corrections and then it goes to the publisher."

"It is very exciting, Papa, and I am sure this one is the best you have ever written."

"I think your mother would say so and for the first time I have put in the story of how we ran away together."

"Oh, Papa, it will certainly amuse and entrance all your readers."

She remembered what Lady Sarah had said and told him how much she had liked his first book.

"Then we must certainly let her have a copy of this one once it is published. Of course I would like to meet her, if it is ever possible."

"Perhaps it will be some time – " Neisa answered vaguely.

The Vicar looked at his watch.

"The Harrisons have just produced a new baby and I promised I would look in to see them before Evensong. I don't suppose you will be coming to Church tonight."

"No, Papa, I went to Church this morning. It was a beautiful service and the choir sung splendidly."

"That is more than I can say of our choir," sighed the Vicar. "It is not all their fault. I am afraid the organ is breaking down again and the last time it was repaired they said there was nothing more they could do to it."

Neisa knew how much this troubled her father.

She wondered if she could ask Carol to give them a new organ, but thought it would be a mistake.

'No one wants poor relations with their hands out-stretched all the time,' she told herself.

Then she felt a strong sense of guilt because of all the beautiful clothes that Carol had given her.

What they had cost, she was quite sure, would have easily paid for a brand new organ.

But she would certainly have looked very strange at Denholme Park in her own clothes!

No one would have taken her for a rich heiress.

'Money is a huge problem whether you have any or not,' she mused.

She went upstairs to open the spare room for Carol and to make sure the bed was made up.

When she came down it was to find Carol in the kitchen boiling a kettle so that they could have some tea.

"I will do it," insisted Neisa.

"I am keeping myself occupied and actually I am not so helpless that I cannot do the same things as you."

"That is because you are intelligent and not because you have to," Neisa retorted and they both laughed.

The Vicar came back after the Church service was over and they had an early supper.

Carol helped Neisa to cook what was available in the kitchen for their meal.

She thought it was a good thing for her cousin to be active and keep her mind off Sir Peter.

Only when they went upstairs to bed did Carol say,

"It is so kind of you to have me here, Neisa. I am sorry I am such a wet rag, but I am so miserable that it is difficult not to cry."

"You must be brave, Carol, and don't leave us for London too soon."

"I must go to America as soon as I can. I am sure I will find things to do there which will help me forget what has happened to me in England."

"Don't be in a hurry," Neisa persisted. "You know, as you have already suggested, that Lady Margrave will be determined to earn the money your father is paying her as your chaperone and will be producing Dukes and Earls galore."

"In that case, I shall be rude to them!"

"Now that would be a mistake."

Carol gave a little cry,

"I am so miserable I only wish to die."

"You are not to say such things, Carol. It only makes it worse."

She helped Carol undress.

Although she knew that Carol would weep as soon as she left the room, there was nothing she could do.

She went to her bedroom thinking that as Carol was crying for Sir Peter, she was crying for the Marquis.

When she climbed into her bed, she was thinking of how kind he had been to her.

She sent up a prayer to God that he would be safe.

She was no longer there to look after him and he would have to look after himself.

At the same time she could not help hoping that he was missing her.

*

The next morning Neisa went down to breakfast early.

She found Betsy, the woman from the village who came in to clean, had prepared it already.

"You've visitors I hears, miss," remarked Betsy.

"Yes, I am really hoping that Miss Carol will stay for luncheon. So please find us something nice to eat."

"I've a chicken for the Vicar – "

"That is splendid! We will all enjoy it"

Chicken was always a treat at the Vicarage.

Then she thought of all the expensive food they had enjoyed at Denholme Park and Carol would think that in contrast chicken was meagre fare.

When Carol did come downstairs, she was looking pale and there were dark lines under her eyes.

"I am afraid you did not sleep all that well," Neisa said, as she kissed her good morning.

"I don't think I slept at all."

"What I suggest you do now, Carol, is to go to the bottom of the garden where you will find a small summer house. Papa put an old sofa in it which we did not want in the house, but it is still very comfortable."

She smiled at Carol before continuing,

"If you sit there for a while listening to the birds and hearing the water running down through the little cascade Mama made, I am sure you will go to sleep."

"I hope so and thank you, Neisa, for being so kind to me."

She ate no breakfast, but drank a cup of coffee.

Then she left right away, as Neisa had suggested, to the summer house at the bottom of the garden.

It was one of Neisa's favourite places when she had the time and she had often fallen asleep there, because it was so peaceful.

Hannah cleared away the breakfast plates and Neisa started to tidy up the house that seemed to her in somewhat of a mess.

Her father, she had learned from Betsy, had gone out very early as someone had been taken ill on one of the farms, so there was no point in keeping breakfast for him.

Betsy went upstairs to make the beds.

Neisa was reading her father's book in the sitting room when she heard a knock on the front door.

She walked across the hall and opened it.

To her astonishment she found Sir Peter outside.

He was just handing over the reins of his mount to the old man who looked after her father's horse.

When he saw Neisa at the door, Sir Peter took off his hat saying,

"Good morning, Carol. I presume you are staying here with Neisa?"

Neisa drew in her breath.

With an effort she forced herself to reply,

"Will you come into the sitting room, Sir Peter? I have something to tell you."

She thought he looked slightly surprised.

He walked slowly into the hall, put his hat down on the side table and followed Neisa into the sitting room.

"Sheldon told me," he began "that Neisa's father was unwell and she had to return home in a hurry. I cannot understand why she could not have waited until today."

There was a pause and with an effort Neisa stated,

"*I* am Neisa and *Carol* is going back to America."

Sir Peter stared at her as if he did not understand.

"What are you saying?"

"I expect the reason you want to see my cousin is that the Admiralty has accepted your invention."

"That is true. I am extremely excited about it and I believe that Neisa will be too."

"Carol is running away, because she could not bear to tell you the truth about herself and she is desperately, really desperately unhappy."

"I don't understand," replied Sir Peter, still looking perplexed. "You said just now you are Neisa. What do you mean by that?"

"What I mean, Sir Peter, is that I am Neisa Moore, the Vicar's daughter, and this is my home."

She waited and as he did not speak, she continued,

"The girl you thought was Neisa is Carol Waverton, my cousin. We changed places because she was so bored and disgusted by men running after her and trying to marry her entirely for her money."

"So you changed places," repeated Sir Peter, as if he found it all hard to believe.

"She was invited to stay by the Marquis because her father, Mr. Waverton, had been extremely kind to him in America," explained Neisa. "We thought, as we would be meeting different people in a very different environment, it would be a change for Carol from everyone pursuing her just because she is so rich."

Neisa thought Sir Peter drew in his breath.

"Then when you talked to each other and you told her how you always intended to stand on your own feet and you would never marry any woman who is rich, you broke her heart."

Neisa was watching Sir Peter as she spoke.

She thought as she said the last words, he stiffened and pursed his lips together.

Still he said nothing, so she went on,

"Carol has been awake all night crying because she has to leave you. She knows that when you realise who she is, you will never want to see her again. That is exactly why, Sir Peter, if that is really how you feel, it would be unnecessarily cruel and very very unkind to see her now. I think, therefore, you should leave immediately."

"Where is – Carol?" Sir Peter asked.

"She is at the bottom of the garden resting in our summer house and because she has been crying all night, I hope she has fallen asleep."

She thought Sir Peter still looked indecisive, so she added quickly,

"Surely you are being very stupid, even though you have invented something brilliant that has been accepted by the Admiralty – "

"Stupid?" Sir Peter challenged sharply.

"You must be aware that what Carol will require if she inherits all the money her father has made, is someone who could organise it for her into the right channels."

She realised that Sir Peter was listening intently.

"No one with any sense would expect someone as delightful and generous as Carol is to be overpowering or possessive about the wealth she does not want and does not like.

"What she needs, and what I hope she will find, is a man who really loves her for herself and who will help her to direct her wealth into projects that will benefit the whole community."

She took a deep breath.

"Children, old people, those who are sick, all need help, as well as all those who are clever but who have no chance whatsoever of getting what they have invented or written about brought in front of the public."

Now Sir Peter was staring at Neisa.

"All that is required is someone with imagination

and brains to do this for Carol, so that she can concentrate on what she loves and what she really wants out of life."

"And what does she want?" he asked in a voice that sounded a little unsteady.

"Carol told me this morning that what she desires more than anything else in the world is to have a beautiful house like yours where she can make a wonderful home for her husband – and her children."

She spoke the last words rather breathlessly.

Sir Peter rose to his feet and Neisa thought he was going to stump out as she had advised.

He walked across the room to the door and turned back to face Neisa.

"You said the summer house is at the bottom of the garden?"

"As far as you can walk – "

She thought he smiled at her and then he was gone.

For a moment she felt exhausted with the effort of speaking to him.

She was uncertain as to whether he was horrified at what she had said or had understood and accepted it.

She could only pray that if he loved Carol enough, he would ask her to marry him.

Money or no money, it would be a triumph for love that she had always believed conquered all obstacles.

She now went into the hall, feeling that she must busy herself rather than sit wondering what was happening.

She put on an apron over the front of her dress and started to brush the carpet as it was stained with mud from her father's boots.

She brushed it away and created rather a dust as she did so.

Then once again there was a knock on the door.

She opened it a little impatiently.

To her utter astonishment it was not the postman as she had expected.

It was *the Marquis*.

He was standing there looking very handsome and somewhat overpowering in his riding clothes.

It took her a second to realise that the old groom was leading another horse away from the front door to the stable.

"Good morning," the Marquis began. "You look a little surprised to see me."

"I – am very – surprised."

The Marquis walked into the hall.

He put his riding whip and his hat down on a chair.

As he did so, Neisa pushed the broom in her hand into the corner and took off her apron.

Then she turned and walked ahead of the Marquis into the sitting room knowing that he would follow her.

She saw him glance round.

Because she felt so nervous, her voice trembled and she stuttered a little as she asked him,

"W-why are y-you h-here?"

"I came here to see Neisa, and I was not in the least surprised when *Neisa* opened the door!"

Neisa stared at him.

"Why do – you call me – that name?"

"Because I realised directly after you had left that I had been stupid. I had thought it strange that your cousin Carol could speak Arabic."

He paused for a moment.

"It was only when Aunt Sarah was telling me how much she had enjoyed your father's book, *Journey's End*, that I realised as he had spent a long time in Africa with his wife and daughter, she would recognise a Berber when she met one and also understood what he was saying."

Neisa, now having difficulty in breathing, replied in a jerky little voice,

"So then – you guessed that – Carol and I – had changed places."

"I also realised that only someone who had moved among the Arab tribes in the East would recognise a drug-addict."

"Please try to understand, my Lord, that I have been extremely angry with myself – for being so foolish. I am so sorry we deceived you. It was only because – Carol was so upset by everyone making such a fuss about her money and men asking her to marry them, not because they loved her but because they wanted to get their greedy hands on the millions she owned."

"I can now appreciate why you so enjoyed dancing on Saturday night as you had not been to many balls."

"It is the very first ball – I have ever attended," she murmured blushing

He smiled.

"Then it must certainly not be the last!"

Neisa made a helpless gesture with her hands.

"If you have read Papa's book, my Lord, you will be aware of how poor we are and how it would have been impossible for me to go to any ball. Even if I was asked to one, I could not afford a gown. The clothes I was wearing when I was staying with you were given to me by Carol."

"I noticed that too and because you were pretending to be her, you were more dressed up than you need have been. I like you just as you are now."

Neisa gave a little chuckle.

"This dress is also one Carol has given me. It was one of hers that she had no further use for."

"You look very lovely in it and now I have another thing to tell you which is why I came here today."

"What is that?" Neisa asked nervously.

"I think it is something that will be a relief to you as it is to me."

The Marquis spoke very seriously.

Neisa looked at him wide-eyed.

"Early this morning the two men I sent to London to escort Randolph abroad returned to Denholme Park. I was surprised to see them back so soon as I had given them strict instructions to travel with him to Rotterdam. And to stay with him even longer if he was not capable of looking after himself."

"What – happened?"

Neisa feared that Randolph had escaped and once again he would be trying to murder the Marquis.

"When they arrived at Tilbury, Randolph was still only semi-conscious, but they managed to drag him to his feet and he walked with them on board. They booked three cabins adjacent to each other. One of my men was paying for them when Randolph suddenly spoke up more or less coherently.

"'Where are we going', he asked. 'We are going to Rotterdam, sir', the man replied, 'and from there you can go anywhere you wish in the world as long as you do not return to England.'"

The Marquis paused for a moment.

"I was told that Randolph stared at him as if for the first time he understood that he was being sent permanently into exile. Then unexpectedly he rushed out of the Purser's Office and onto the deck."

Neisa was listening breathlessly.

"It took a second or two for the two men to follow him and they noticed when they did so that he had thrust something into his mouth. Then as one of them put out his hand to pull him back inside the office, he jumped over the railing and into the sea!"

Neisa gave an exclamation of horror.

"It was then they realised he had taken the poison pill he carried in his pocket and which had been intended for me. He had taken his own life. It took some time to retrieve the body.

"Even if Randolph had not taken the pill, he would anyway have drowned."

The Marquis finished speaking and Neisa gave a little cry.

"It – sounds a wrong thing to say," she murmured, "but I am very glad that I need no longer – be afraid that he will come back and try to kill you,"

"I must admit," the Marquis said quietly, "that he will not be missed."

"Now you will – be safe, and that is what – really matters."

"I hoped you would feel like that, but tell me why."

Neisa did not understand his question and looked up at him.

"I was going to ask you, Neisa, to look after me," the Marquis continued, "and to protect me from Randolph. Now I know I want you for a very different reason."

"What can – that be?"

"I want you with me. To talk to me, to inspire me and to make me happy."

The Marquis spoke quietly and for a moment she did not understand.

Then he smiled.

"I am now asking you, my dearest darling one, to *marry* me. For I know in my heart that I just cannot live without you."

"It – cannot be true – " whispered Neisa.

"Let me explain it in a different way – "

The Marquis put his arms around her as he spoke and drew her close to him.

Then his lips were on hers.

At first it was the same gentle kiss he had given her the night he thanked her for saving his life.

When once again he could feel the innocence and sweetness of her lips, a feeling he had never experienced in his life swept over him.

He knew that this was everything he had ever been seeking and what he had been longing to find.

It was the purest love that Neisa had shown him came from the heart and the soul.

It was something so precious and so wonderful that he knew it was more important than all the treasures and riches of the world.

He went on kissing her and felt her body melt into his.

He knew they were one person rather than two and he would never lose her again.

Neisa felt as if the skies had opened and the sun and the moon had fallen at her feet.

The Marquis's kiss was as unbelievably wonderful as she remembered it and a thousand times more.

It made her feel as if he was carrying her into the burning heat of the sun.

The Light of Love was shining within both of them and came from Heaven itself.

When the Marquis raised his head, she murmured,

"I love you, I adore you, but I thought that I would never see you again."

"Why should you think so?" asked the Marquis and his voice was a little unsteady.

"How can you marry the daughter of a Vicar? You ought to marry someone much more important."

"There just could never be anyone more important in my life than you, my darling Neisa, and that is the truth. I have been searching for you all my life, but I believed I would never find you."

He kissed her forehead tenderly.

"I want you, my lovely one, not only to protect me from any more harm I may come to, but to make our lives together perfect and exquisite."

Neisa made a little murmur of happiness.

"Even to see us," he added, "will make other people feel happier and will then want to do more for the world around them."

He drew in his breath.

"No other woman has made me feel like this, but you are *so* different. I think in all sincerity that God has brought you to me."

"I am sure that is true," Neisa whispered, "and I am so incredibly lucky to have found you as you are the most glorious, marvellous man that ever existed."

The Marquis laughed.

"I hope you will always think so and I will try very hard to live up to what you think of me."

He kissed her again.

Now his kisses became possessive and passionate. He knew, as he felt her whole body respond, that there was so much he had to teach her about love.

They both realised that their love was Divine.

It was completely different from the love that most people found in their lives.

As the Marquis now looked down at Neisa's sweet, unspoilt and untouched beauty, he knew how supremely fortunate he was.

How few men ever found the true 'Holy Grail' they all seek, that is the love which can only come from God.

It was a long time later that Neisa sighed,

"I wonder what Sir Peter has said to Carol."

"Is Peter here?" the Marquis asked. "I thought it was where he might be. When he had learned this morning your cousin had left, I have never seen a man look more worried and concerned."

"So you told him where you thought Carol would be?"

"He was asking for 'Neisa', but I was determined to keep that particular young lady for myself!"

Neisa slipped her hand into his.

"Yours completely and absolutely," she murmured. "But I am still afraid I am dreaming."

"We will dream together, my darling. Shall we go and look for the young lovers or just leave them where they are?"

Neisa smiled at him.

"I want to be alone with you and I am sure that if Sir Peter was leaving Carol because he could not face all the money she has, he would have gone by now."

"He would be a big fool to do anything so stupid. If you owned all the riches in the world, I would still want nothing but you – and *you* alone."

"And that is what you have. Just *me* and I am very poor!"

"That's just *your* description, but to me you are the richest person in the world because of your brain, which is so quick and perceptive and has saved me twice. And your heart, which is larger than anyone else's I have ever known and will embrace not only me but everyone you come into contact with."

He stopped speaking to smile at her lovingly.

"Last of all my precious Neisa, you have a soul. A soul that is beautiful, inspiring and perfect. To me you are not only a woman but an angel come down from Heaven."

There were tears in Neisa's eyes as she flung her arms round his neck.

"I love you, I adore you!" she cried. "Please go on loving me like this for ever and ever."